ANISE
BOY

The Seeds of Life

In 1946, Anise Boy is just a 5-year-old boy observing his mother and other women diligently harvesting anise in his Syrian village. The scene provides his first glimpse into the world around him. The Roma, called gypsies then, often roam from village to village at the end of harvest season to perform their mesmerizing acts and acrobatics.

Changing Tides

Following several years of drought, the boy's father advises him to venture from his small village to learn the trade of tailoring in nearby Damascus. Meanwhile, the young boy keeps reading and writing as a backup plan.

Sewing Destiny

In his early teens, he finds a tailoring job in a bustling workplace with dozens of young women. Soon, he finds himself emotionally entangled in this enchanting atmosphere.

Compare and Contrast

He can't help but compare the village girls from home with the new city girls he meets; he notices their differences in work ethic, behavior, and all aspects of life.

The Blossoming Heart

His emotions bloom beyond what his mind could fathom, leading him on a remarkable journey exploring what loves looks like. He discovers that love itself is an eternal search.

The novel was revised and translated through a collaboration between the author Hsain Warour and the translation department at Khayat Publishing House. Additionally, both internal and external designs for the novel were created by the design team at Khayat.

ANISE BOY

First published in 2024

ISBN: 978-1-961420-29-8

Copyright © Hsain Warour 2023

Library of Congress Control Number: 2023952608

KHAYAT

WASHINGTON, DC
UNITED STATES

www.khayatpublishing.com

HSAIN WAROUR

ANISE BOY

An eternal search for love

To

Anise Girls

*You must forget who you are, or close your eyes and
shield your heart from what you see;
but you cannot.*

CHAPTER ONE

1946
Full Orchestra

The women working the anise field. The forewoman. The small sickles with resonance. The scent of grass, virgin soil, and the fragrance of Eve.

Nature and its vocabulary: The breezes of the season. The music of water. The birds' singing on nearby and distant trees. The roar of underground water pumps. Murmurs of farmers far and near, men and women. An existential symphony for human meteorites that only means life passed by here one day.

This story—people, land, and spring—is ruled by the seasons of anise, when everyone without exception eagerly awaited it—from young children exchanging anise for paper planes, cotton candy, and sweets.

The forewoman's call to my mother, among the women weeding the anise, "Bring your gear and come! We are sitting under the almond tree waiting for you!"

The forewoman interrupts the scene, stops the performance. I was like the forewoman's doll that day. She jokingly asked me to choose a woman I liked from the field. With the possessiveness of childhood, I told her: "I like them all!" They laughed at my innocent answer a long time. The forewoman said to my mother, "Watch out for him. My son was like him; I lost him because of love."

I notice a butterfly hovering. I jump like a monkey and start chasing. It disappears among plants, just like every beautiful thing that arouses our desires vanishes.

Night comes and I can only count the stars, scattered around the moon, that never leave their eternal positions. They suffer agony and confusion, as legends say, like the Canopus.

My mother wraps herself in my father's cloak. I fall asleep on her hand, full of anise fragrance. I hear my father's voice in the morning, from somewhere I do not know. Here I am starting a new day, wild, full of wonder and boundless naughtiness.

Once, I asked my mother: "How did I come into this world?"

"From a cabbage head!" she said.

"Who brought that cabbage head?"

"The girls who worked with us, weeding and harvesting anise."

This is how I came into the world, into a place I did not choose. I was given a name without my permission, like most males in our village. Usually, you would be named after your grandfather, a spiritual homage seeking continuity, tradition, and inheritance, a connection to your origin. These concepts do not hold meaning for the child who arrives in the world crying—seeking nothing more than fulfillment of desires and needs.

My first realizations during the childhood I never had, drowned me in an anxiety difficult to comprehend, making my surroundings appear gelatinous. Over time, I became certain it was not like that; rather, it was quite the opposite. The issue lay within me and not my surroundings, as if I were born with the magic carpet inside instead of beneath me. It's as if my father planted this carpet's seed within my mother's womb—I mean, within the cabbage head.

As I grew, this carpet expanded colorfully and ornamentally, contributing to my desire to move from one place to another. It sailed with me and my lightweight belongings, leaning whichever direction my head inclined – whether from coercion or desire or even obsession with something yet undiscovered. Was it the pleasure of exploration and knowing what lay beyond the narrow circle where I'd spent the first years of life? My village lacked even a specific identity as a place beyond the anise until its history came along.

In that place, no more than a speck of dust to the universe, Um Barjas cut my umbilical cord. She threw me into the arms of a mother whose frail body could not withstand the harshness of life in a village where night bridged day, working in fields, orchards, and tending livestock.

One spring, she gave birth to a firstborn who wasn't destined to live. Then, I arrived in that cabbage head. My sister followed and lived until 13 years old, succumbing to typhoid fever exactly one year after our mother succumbed to asthma.

My mother's doctor was a nomadic woman who left her tents, wilderness, and stars to join her husband in tending goats for farmers in the village. Her husband preferred the shade of orchards, water channels, and stability over the open air and life of a nomad. Yet my soul craved just what he ran away from.

My mother's dream was also to see me far from seasonal nothings, away from the cycle of erosion and misery of working on land that stole her life and hindered progress in people's lives around her. She wanted to see me settled as a tailor, her now fading eyes watching me ride my bicycle toward town to learn the tailoring profession without severing my connection to the land completely. In the fields, I assisted my father during the remaining daylight hours and occasional evenings.

The Young Ones Grow Up

As in our sleeping dreams, our waking dreams were also vivid. We granted our dreams and imagination the possibilities of reality rather than dreams developing our reality. My mother explained many of her childhood dreams, as she wished she could be one day, while looking at me and hiding her sorrows, which turned into tears wiped away by the tip of her headscarf, that she would wear tightly on her head when she suffered a headache. She recounted her nightmares, too.

Slowly, I discovered the night conceals shadows formed during the day. And I learned mirages are not only seen by desert nomads. My heart perceived what my eyes could not see. I'll leave the name of my village, as written in my diary like a wind-tilted signpost, where all roads lead to Damascus.

I was as pure as clear water when I told my friend Hamza, longing for that moment to return: Temporary creatures, you and I, and all those who inhabit this place will one day become memories in the logbook of time. Many have lived here before us, perhaps for thousands of years. No one can recall the exact truth of the past with its shining face. If you ask a thousand people to describe how they witnessed the sun rising at the same moment, you would be amazed at what you hear. Each person will describe their own sun—here lies the truth. Our minds are controlled by fatigue, anticipation for seasons, and false promises of better prices for our village's anise crops from unseen merchants next season. Always next season, they say.

We see only two who claim to compete in raising its price; the truth is they are two links in a single chain that only raises our hopes, a chain that starts at the Tower of Babel and ends at our slanted towers of destiny here and now.

What can one expect from those who work day and night? All their words—arguments, fights, reconciliations, and reproductions—from the language do not exceed a hundred words. A meager menu in spite of dialects rich with Lebanese, Palestinian, Sammaq Mountain, Yemeni, Iraqi, Egyptian, Hejazi, and

Maghrebi accents. One can recognize the roots of each family by hearing a few words from any of its members.

Everyone in our village is illiterate except for one individual on whom we all rely for reading and replying to messages. However, these messages come from only five villagers who escaped to Argentina for fear of being drafted into the Ottoman army. Even the village chief appointed by the French mandate government can neither read nor write. He was provided a seal as his signature for official documents.

Guests in Light Shades

Yes, my mother is in a big house, a house for more than one family. My mother, like a feather from a wounded bird, leaves the courtyard where imagination can play and clings to the iron bars of her wedding room window. Asthma drains the life within her as she stubbornly hits her head against the iron bars; if these bars had a heart, her pain would melt it.

Her pleas to God, His prophets, and His saints quickened her steps toward salvation from this world, which provided her a husband who could only steal time for rest and romance in their mud home on land—like all farms in the village—designated for the Ottoman Sultan.

It was September, leaves beginning to wither during the Feast of the Cross, when my mother left nothing for us but a garment worn through every season, hung by a nail on a wall, giving birth to creatures belonging to a time other than her own in its shadow. The dry wall of mud absorbed the scent of her motherhood and the lingering aroma of anise from her clothing.

The big house is metaphorically big. In reality, it is nothing more than bedrooms for strangers arriving from distant villages as guests or wanderers on life's path or those who have nowhere else to go, a refuge like other "big houses" in other villages.

Our house and our neighbor Badran's house welcomed six Armenian families who had survived genocide at the hands of the Ottomans. My uncle spoke about those Armenians who lived in our house: Musa, Azniv, and Arten. He described their high morals, their skill in repairing farming tools, and their trustworthiness. He then talked about how they eventually moved on to Damascus, Aleppo, and Beirut looking for work or a reunion with family from different Armenian regions.

As time went by, this sad Armenian story stuck in my head. This led me to learn the profession of tailoring under the kind and mature Armenian, Wahram

Shahbandarian, in Damascus. His son Aro, is still my friend, and I visit him at his shop in Damascus. To this day, he is the most famous hat tailor around!

Ephemeral Creatures

When the village elders gathered in one of their homes, they were quickly drawn to their past by its golden threads, connecting them to their roots. I bet none of them knew their true origin or the purity of their lineage they would boast about. No human lineage on earth is entirely pure. Wars, invasions, conquests, and all that accompanied them—including captives, prisoners, sexual assaults, migrations—all have given human beings genetic modifications beyond imagination.

—

A prominent villager refused to accept that his family's roots were impure until his family tried to keep an unexpected secret. A girl in his family became pregnant by a young man. This scandal spread among the women initially and eventually reached the father of the pregnant girl's family. The story, a spreading fire, was temporarily smothered but later rekindled.

A nearby farm's guard discovered the mutilated body of a young man with his severed penis in his mouth. The victim was the man who got the girl pregnant. Many in shock, the village divided into attackers and defenders who went to battle. People on both sides were injured and the split lasted decades. The fires of revenge and passion did not calm until they claimed the bitter harvest of innocent blood.

The victim's brother was one of the five people who'd gone to Argentina. The lack of contact and illiteracy made it a challenge to let him know about his brother's death. When he eventually returned and learned the shocking news about his brother, he regretted not sending letters from Argentina.

Although most of his family disagreed, he believed reconciliation with the guilty family was best. A foggy atmosphere surrounded the village as revenge   prevailed.

In a small village where everyone knows one another, how many seasons of anise have passed to fully pay the price in this case of blood? During peace, it seemed like one home uniting villagers who were one family trying to raise enough to serve the financial sentence for murder.

Who would pay the price of revenge in such an atmosphere? Only those who dare to grasp the stick from the middle, risk open-minded moderation in the heat of extremism. Despite others' opinions, the brother of the victim secretly visited a prominent member of a neutral family to seek advice about his family, still adamant about seeking revenge.

—

A refugee from Lebanon who had sought shelter in our village once told me about witnessing soil where love might not grow:

"After living in this village for a while and now losing my loved one for whom I came here, I can't imagine life here anymore. So, I must leave reluctantly. Life among you is harsh."

CHAPTER TWO

Low-Lying Land

We did not live our childhood as we should have. Distance had an effect, so did the roads and the waiting. Our childhood yearned for escape, even into the unknown, or it sought calculated adventure and discovery, written on the pages of fear from our father, the clergyman, the afterlife, the jinn, the ghosts of night and nightmares. Our wakeful dreams didn't go beyond Bu Louai's canal and the two mills in the village, its cemetery, its water channels, its Roman tunnels, and what came before them.

Children grow up.

The circle of place expands and distance takes on a different dimension. It was rare for me to agree with the neighborhood children on adventures beyond those fenced-in and marked by cemeteries, jinn, wolves, stray dogs, and older mischievous children. Most of the time, I chose to go alone and returned pondering my memory's reservoirs and imaginations drawn from previous terrifying experiences.

We grew up in a void filled with illusions of a comfortable life. We grew up barefoot except for little sandals or long lightweight shirts, resembling adults' jalabiyas, covering our nakedness. We wore them over dirt in every season.

My uncle Ali takes me with him to the Baik's farm—arriving through its western gate. Together, we enter a shed with an uncovered red tractor. He lifts me upon its bonnet between two bars protecting me from falling and then climbs behind the steering wheel—the tractor roars. I laugh for no reason. I might be the first child in the village granted this great honor and will boast of it for years among fellow children.

It didn't take long for things to reach this point. My uncle promised to photograph me behind the wheel of a tractor as if I were driving it. Within a week, he used a black, box-shaped Kodak camera. I cherished the photo for more than three years, sharing it with children and adults alike. A second photo shows him preparing the field for sowing anise. In a third photo, I chase butterflies after the anise blooms. A fourth picture features young women harvesting the crop among anise flowers, with their songs carried by summer breezes to a distant water channel where shepherds rest and play melancholic tunes on reeds.

The first savings from my apprenticeship, as a tailor, went toward a camera, the same Kodak model, and that's when my hobby began. However, that interest soon gave way to capturing moments through mental images. The eye of memory eagerly snapped countless pictures of captivating landscapes, faces, architecture, and reflections.

My time also revolved around the home sewing machine my mother bought me with the money she saved while I learned tailoring. She loved watching me work, saying it brought her peace. Truthfully, she wanted to ensure I would be fine before her illness eventually took her away. Her last wish was for me to gift the sewing machine to my sister on her wedding day, when I could afford a bigger one.

As I grew older, so did my ability to discern between good and bad, beauty and ugliness, kindness and malice. I became disinterested in greedy and self-serving individuals. They reminded me of invasive plants or harmful insects wreaking havoc on their environment. Their actions had devastating consequences not just for individuals, but entire regions where inhabitants had lived peacefully for centuries. My interest in them is not pity or sympathy. My attention isn't focused on blaming them because it does no good now—the dead cannot be brought back to life. Instead, I want to show their actions amidst the passage of time. Let time judge for the wounds they caused—wounds that bleed decades later. In their time, they turned others into temporary entities, fit only for enslavement and short-term consumption. Yet sometimes not everything known should be spoken.

Many people came to the village as if it were prey, or like a cow that needed to be slaughtered. Large farms of wealthy landowners spread around its outskirts. The increase in its population was clearly visible as people migrated for work in the capital or government jobs.

Add to this growth what was never expected. The village was, and still is, like a low-lying land where any description suitable for a village crowded with those seeking quick wealth applies. Real estate is its most prominent feature. Dozens of thriving real estate offices are scattered in all its corners, not to mention brokers operating from their homes. There is no monitoring or accountability for this parasitic profession, which emerged in the first half of the 1950s.

In our village, a popular saying goes, "Low-lying land absorbs its water and others' water."

CHAPTER THREE

Monkey's Anklets 1947

The night before the Feast of the Cross, we were eager as children to wake up in the morning to wear our new clothes and shoes. As I walked out of the alley to the meadow separating my house from our neighbor's, I saw a group of Ghajer setting up their tents. Some passersby would stop for a moment to watch before continuing on their way.

The villagers were accustomed to seeing the Ghajer settle on the village meadows after the harvest seasons. Their activities varied between pre-harvest and post-harvest. Initially, they carried sieves, rakes, sifters, protective leather that shielded them from the summer sun, and water containers with hemp threads, needles, and combs made of bone—often used for treating lice. Women carried kohl-liners for their eyes. During post-harvest, they would make gold teeth and engage in begging, as people were wealthier after harvesting seasons.

I saw a Ghajer girl inside a tent that had been set up before I arrived, feeding a monkey through the opening. Later, I noticed two Ghajer men tying a thick rope to the house of my neighbors, Bargis and Shihad. Confused, I asked Bargis what the two men planned to do with this rope.

The Ghajer girl Zeina will walk on it!

I proceeded to imagine a woman walking on a rope. Then I returned from my wandering to see what they were doing. They had set up three tents. I saw a young Ghajer man carrying a drum, moving from one tent to another. He looked at me and greeted me in a way that pleased me: he curled his fist and beat the drum strongly, twice. These beats were invitations for the neighborhood children, and the neighborhoods that heard the drum. The drummer entered the middle tent and closed it behind him.

I turned my gaze to the girl's tent with the monkey, which was also closed. My neighborhood friends had gathered: Ayoub, Abdo, Farhan, Ibrahim, Naim, and Hamza arrived from farther neighborhoods. We all stood close together on the edge of the canal.

My eyes followed the girl as she moved from one tent to another. I did not see the monkey when she opened the tent and came out. I noticed her dress, a bright, dominant orange, that almost touched the ground. In contrast to the sunlight, it appeared transparent. I could see her legs map up to her thighs.

She tied her hair with a yellow handkerchief. My eyes shifted to an older girl who came out of the third tent holding a teapot. She quickly set up an outdoor stove using two stones from behind the tent and gathered dry straw next to our neighbor Bergus' wall. A young man also came from the third tent carrying firewood. She lit a fire in the stove, and then the monkey emerged from its tent.

It seemed the monkey had taken advantage of their absence and came toward us, so we ran away in fear. We climbed onto the nearest rooftop overlooking the Peder farm field to watch what was happening. Everything seemed a riddle, and anticipation dominated that day.

Under a scorching sun, on the rooftop of our shed that overlooks the courtyard, we sat, watching and waiting. In the afternoon, the drummer emerged from the central tent wearing a different outfit. He was dressed completely in silk: a tailored shirt, red trousers, and a white silk headdress with long tassels, which I had never seen in the village apart from on the district governor.

The drummer passionately played; his drum's powerful beat undoubtedly reached every house in the village and everyone working in the far-off fields. People of all ages gathered around the space the Ghajer designated for their performances; however, women went to the houses surrounding the courtyard instead— ours being one of them. Most family women gathered on our rooftop where they could not be seen by others.

The celebration began with a young girl in traditional dance attire moving to the Ghajer melodies. The flute player's tune enchanted everyone. It was apparent she would become an accomplished dancer. She swayed and quivered, her provocative movements hinting at sexuality that would not go unnoticed by adolescent boys.

The second act featured a young Ghajer man who emerged from his tent holding a bundle of objects we hadn't seen before. He unfurled the bundle, revealing a white cloth he waved in the air, transforming it into a white dove that flew over spectators' heads. He then performed impressive sleight-of-hand that amazed and garnered multiple rounds of applause.

The third act was so peculiar it captured our attention completely, a silence akin to everyone holding their breath. A young man appeared from the first tent wearing the silk attire of a drummer, playing the drum as he led the monkey. The golden anklets worn by the monkey caught my eye, though in my naivety I didn't realize they were artificial. I told my mother after the festival that the monkey's anklets equaled all the gold worn by women in our village.

The dancer and monkey performed graceful dance movements. I was surprised by how differently they danced than people in our village. The Ghajer man danced in an extraordinary way, occasionally imitating the monkey's actions, which seemed to pester some onlookers, as if trying to meddle with their clothes or hair. The final act began as the dancer and monkey stood alongside the spectators.

The drummer and flute player entered the scene. The sound of the drum vibrated, almost masking the melody played by the flutist. Zeina, the Ghajer matron, emerged from her tent and made her way toward the tightrope starting point, near a beggar's house. A storm of applause. She paid no attention to anyone as the anklets on her feet jingled. The drummer stopped performing, while the flutist continued a dance tune. He followed her in a gentle swaying dance, as if saying to spectators, "Wait for the magic." He stood under the first part of the tightrope, bowed, and then advanced to a young Ghajer man I had never seen before.

He clasped his hands in front of the bent young man. The dancer Zeina lifted her apricot silk dress this time, with a shawl like a cloud of sugar. She ascended from one young man's hands to another's back and then onto the tightrope.

The rope vibrated as she stood on it, looking like a palm tree. She greeted the spectators with her hands. An old Ghajer man, whom I hadn't seen yet, came with what looked like a spear raised towards Zeina. She took it, raising it high, then held it horizontally before her waist and began walking the rope. Another wave of applause. She moved her feet cautiously, and with each step, my chest tightened in fear she might fall. The rope was about four meters high. Her fall would mean injury, if not disaster. She wore golden silk pants under her dress, different from what our women wear. Her anklets no longer carried as much importance to me as those cautious steps.

A young man made room for me and my cousin Ayoub to see. He lifted me for a better view. The Ghajer Zeina noticed us; perhaps she thought the young man who lifted me was waving, so she greeted him with a strong nod followed by a wink that made him lift me higher until I felt like I would slip from his grasp.

I realized everything Zeina did in those moments was for him. Zeina reached the end of the rope, stopping near Bergus' house for a moment, her eyes fixed on the young man who held me. I thought she was also smiling at me. With additional delight, my little heart flit between my ribs with both admiration and fear for her safety. I imagined what might happen if she were to fall and how I would react. I silently prayed it wouldn't. Her glances began making me believe all of this was for me, and me alone.

The monkey was preparing to jump onto the rope. However, Zeina gestured with her hand to stop it. The monkey backed away and returned to its trainer. Zeina performed stunts that made me cover my eyes with my hands, fearing a painful surprise.

My father's hand nudged me from behind, indicating I should follow him, but I didn't respond. He came back a little while later; by then, the monkey had jumped onto the rope and swung from it to the ground or to Zeina's shoulder. Sometimes, it would stand in front of a spectator to perform a provocative move before heading back to the rope. Zeina stepped off the rope, and the flute player and drummer approached her, providing a lively tune for her to dance.

This time, my father's hand firmly nudged me before gripping my neck tightly. He led me out of the celebration as joyous sounds continued echoing in my head. We passed by the Ghajer's donkeys tied behind Abu Majid's house and walked towards our northern threshing ground. There, I helped my father by holding the burlap sack for him to fill with leftover grains mixed with dirt – which we usually scattered for the hens cared for by my mother and aunt in our courtyard.

—

Everything I had seen from that day accompanied me in my waking dream and then my sleep. The monkey played with me. Zeina carried me to the rope and taught me how to walk on it with balance, saving me from falling many times. I invited her to come with me to our house so my mother and aunt could see her. She accepted. The drummer and the piper followed, and our yard filled with people. My father came from outside the house, grabbed me by the ear this time, and rubbed it. I screamed, waking up terrified. My mother's hand wiped the sweat dripping down my forehead.

The joys of the Ghajer were imprinted in my memory: the sound of their drums, their pipes, their dancing, the smoke rising before their tents, their travels taking me into their world and open spaces that revealed the secrets of their experiences acquired over hundreds, if not thousands of years.

My memory only calmed for a moment before repeating all these images again: Zeina, the monkey, the drummer, the flute player, and the little girl who had opened the celebration in our village. All of this meant nothing to my father except for the threshing season.

CHAPTER FOUR

**She dragged her shadow with her and disappeared.
I wished that even her shadow would
remain on the ground.**

That year's season wasn't quite right and the Eid holidays were approaching. Many concerns slept within my head, or lay dormant—similar to that which nature grants its trees. It was not a satisfactory state of mixed shapes and colors; upon waking, I could not distinguish between light and darkness, solid and liquid, faith and darkness. This and other paradoxes and contradictions persisted.

From early childhood through my adulthood, I didn't recall the sun ever rising before me. I always woke before dawn; I recognized the shapes of resident birds and those migrating through God's space in search of sustenance and safety. The local ones coexisted with people, living right alongside them. They built their nests in the roofs of their houses and the trees of their orchards. With heightened intuition, they knew friends and enemies. They differentiated between the stingy and the generous, recognized places, and discerned between a stick and a hunting rifle.

My father, who was not sorry for escaping life due to its bitterness, would rise from sleep after me. He headed to his beloved mare's stable, always pampering her. He saddled her tenderly, talking to her as if she were a lover. He cleaned her body from head to hoof, and washed her feeding trough as well. He would go into the hay storage and occasionally mix straw with our home's wheat supply. He provided her with fresh water and drank from the same container himself. This daily ritual took place before he washed his face, as if it were an obligation akin to worship.

I loved the blonde mare, perhaps more than my father. I secretly learned to ride even though my mother warned me not to mount her and threatened to tell my father. She considered my learning at such a young age mischievous. I had to ride bareback, because I couldn't lift a saddle onto her back. I rode freely, without reins.

In the wilderness, she pulled away like the wind, as if she was in her own space, firmly believing I was a cavalier and could keep up with her. Yet one day I fell. She kept running more than 100 meters. Then, she stopped and looked toward me. I writhed in pain. She neighed wildly and returned. With the tenderness of a mother, she nuzzled me with her muzzle to ensure my safety. Her tears—perhaps due to guilt—streamed down my face.

I regained my determination. I got up and mounted her again to return home. Yet she refused my strong desire to gallop, as I nudged her with the heels of my small feet. Instead, she walked quietly. Upon reaching the house, she neighed joyfully, a sound I will never forget, as if she was announcing the arrival of a groom.

My father knew this secret, and he kept it to himself, believing I would learn a life lesson.

One day, I silently led the mare from the stable. I took her on a longer gallop than usual. She made her own paths. She stopped at a pile of stones and began digging the ground with her front legs. She let out a neigh I had never heard before. My hands' hitting, my legs' kicking, and the rein's stinging could not move her.

I left the place without any suspicion of her sudden stubbornness, thinking she might just be thirsty or hungry. Later, while telling one of the elders about my skill in controlling her reins and riding her without a bridle, I narrated my fall. I spoke about her sharp neigh at that pile of stones. I realized she had stopped and stood still at the site of my fall. The man appeared pensive and said with a mix of doubt and certainty, "Horses only behave this way in certain situations— when they sense bloodshed."

—

That year, the rain was scarce. The water levels in the wells plummeted. We needed more water to grow anise, so we didn't plant that season. Trees withered. No girls were weeding or singing, and neither did the harvesters in the fields. With our pantry emptied of grain, we made our bread from barley mixed with a bit of wheat or corn. The mare became an unbearable burden. Severe conversations erupted between my father and mother over the mare, leading to a simmering resentment that nearly resulted in divorce on more than one occasion.

They remained on opposite sides, every time the subject of selling the mare came up.

My father yelled at my mother, "I won't let anyone ride her after me!"

My mother refused to submit to his arrogance. "Oh, Antara; she needs barley but we need it more!" she said.

Things escalated. My aunt intervened. My mother would never accept my father's opinion, becoming more defensive and fierce. One dawn he woke anxiously and headed to the stable in the courtyard to prepare the mare. Angrily, my mother threw off her bed cover and caught him.

"What's going on?" she asked. "I see you've prepared the mare. Where are you off to?"

Without turning toward her, he answered in a broken voice, "To the market."

"What market?" she asked apprehensively.

"The horse markets," he said in a voice she could barely hear.

"What are you saying? The horse markets!?"

She tried to snatch the mare's reins from his tight grip but her slender fingers couldn't untangle them. A silence reigned.

"The holiday is in a few days," he said. "How else will we celebrate?"

Her fingers loosened. A momentary triumph began to appear on his face. It was soon followed by tears in my mother's eyes.

"But you'll regret it," she said.

The Eid holidays of the poor, the hungry, and the deprived are not like the ones marked on a calendar. This time, I did not hesitate. I cried all the way from home to the horse market, when my father sat me behind him, on his blond mare. She walked us— unaware of where we headed—under a row of walnut trees surrounding the land of El-Dar orchard, which had been the "pillar of light" for the rebellious Prince Abdelkader El Djezairi (Abu Mehiddin) for more than a century and a half ago, when he was exiled from Algeria to this place. I used to imagine a shadow of a prince there, and later I saw the image of the new owner of Karm El-Dar's land, the ownership of the property transferred to him.

We were still at the beginning of the road, heading toward the horse market in Damascus. To our left, a vast stretch of barren land devoid of trees, offered a full view of Mount Qasioun and its majestic presence. We passed a white stone villa belonging to a Moroccan doctor, whose grandfather accompanied Prince Abdelkader on his exile journey and was granted this land. He was a skilled photographer. Some of the photos he took of the landmarks of my village are still in their possession. He had a servant named Saleem who spoke in Moroccan dialect, using many words we couldn't understand.

On our right, a villa belonging to an advisor to the king. He had purchased a quarter of the village's lands from the heirs of Prince Abdelkader, along with its spring water nurturing all our village's land.

The mare took us along a line of almond trees bordering Ismail Al-Maliki's ancient grapevine. It is enough to say "the Effendi" to refer to that man who still shines in the memory of the village. Not because he was a feudal lord affected by agricultural reform laws or because he was once president of Damascus' chamber of agriculture, but for his helping hands that alleviated much suffering throughout the village. He, too, had bought a quarter of the village's lands with the aforementioned spring water from the heirs of the prince.

The mare took us through vineyards and across properties also sold by Prince Abdelkader's' heirs to two Lebanese men from Deir Al-Qamar. One was killed by his employee from our village over a wage dispute. Everyone knew the murderer could not even afford food for the day—being one of the poorest people in our village.

We left the dirt path and took the Damascus road. After a few miles, we reached the gateway of Al-Midan, known as the "Gateway of God." As we crossed through the Al-Midan neighborhood, the horse's hooves clacked on the paved stones and iron of the tramway tracks. I will never forget the sound. Finally, we entered Bab al-Musalla's horse market.

I spoke at length about our journey to Damascus since no one seems to be interested in writing for memory, and what future days may hold. In the market, my father gripped the horse's rein while my small hand clung to a finger in his other palm. The chilly early morning wind stung, and the tears caused by cold mingled with those falling in sadness for parting with our horse.

I noticed my father's hand lifting the rein, as he discreetly wiped tears off his cheek. Various men came, one after another, to examine our horse. One of them placed his right hand on its flank; she snorted in irritation and eyed him distrustfully. Turning toward my father as if reproaching him for this stranger's actions, she stretched her head toward me and then back to him, rubbing against us both. Another approached and patted its chest; she straightened up before neighing loudly and retreating, causing the man to lose balance and nearly fall.

I noticed a man watching us from amidst a crowd inspecting another horse. He took that horse's rein from its owner's hand, leading it toward us. He passed the horse in front of our mare; she paid no attention to the other horse, solely focused on our presence nearby.

Within moments, three people hovered around us, followed by a few others. They faced us. Another man arrived; they seemed to be working for him. He was the oldest and most elegant, wearing a striped silk jumpsuit with a wide golden silk shawl around his waist. Its tassels dangled on his left side. He wore a red Fez separated from his head by a white mehramah. He signaled to another in the group wearing a vest over a dirty white shirt with soiled cuffs and black pants. The man's head was wrapped in a turban, which looked like Shaziliah style. He approached my father and asked in a whispering voice:

"Does she have her Koshan?" he asked about the horse's ID.

"Including her origin and lineage too!" my father said.

He turned toward the horse, busy shooing a fly hovering around her mane. Then, he looked at me. He put his hand on my head as if offering consolation for the patience I needed.

"How much do you want for her?" the man asked.

"She is not for sale!" my father said.

My heart leaped. It sprouted wings and flew through the village wilderness, while the mare galloped in the infinite space like a dazzling flash. I looked at my father, wiping away tears of happiness with my hands and my sleeve.

"Why are you standing with her in the market then?" asked an elder.

"Is standing in the market forbidden?" my father said.

Another person said, "In the market, you either sell or buy!"

My father said, "Or just watch!"

People exchanged bewildered glances of disappointment. They withdrew while I clung to my father's hand and showered it with kisses.

"Does that mean you're not going to sell the mare?!" I asked.

My father remained silent. My imagination returned from the wilderness to the village celebrating Eid and children playing in the courtyard of a Sufi shrine.

My father's hand tightened around mine, prompting us to exit the market; meanwhile, farmers and merchants continued flocking.

A black carriage stopped at the entrance of the market from the southern side. Its driver, dressed in foreign attire, quickly got out to open its rear door. A man in a gleaming white robe emerged, wearing a red shemagh on his head. They paused briefly by the carriage before the driver gestured toward us. My father gripped the mare's reins, preparing to leave. He shared a long glance with me, conveying resolve. He said, "Follow me!"

The man and his driver approached. They stopped in front of us. The man greeted my father, and the mare stopped. She snorted and began to examine my father.

"Is this mare yours?"

My father nodded.

"Do you sell it?" he asked.

His accent was different from any other Arabic I had heard; I later learned he was from Kuwait.

"This mare is not for sale!" my father said.

The man smiled, sensing the sadness in my father's voice. He spoke warmly, like a brother to another:

"Then I want it as a gift from you."

His eyes watched my father's reaction, already knowing about my father's generosity in such situations. I looked at my father, whose face flushed with blood and emotion. He questioned the man.

"What will you do with the mare?"

"What do you mean?" the man asked.

"I mean, if you intend to trade her, you won't get her!"

"Why would that concern you?"

"I want this mare to live here, give birth here, and die here!"

"If I were one of those people, I wouldn't ask for her as a gift. Rest assured, I am not one of them! I bought a piece of land on the outskirts of Damascus, converted it into a farm. As for the mare, I wish to acquire her as a private possession. I promise that no one but me will touch her!"

My father tried to dispel remaining doubts.

"Where is your farm?"

"To the south of Al-Baridah location; precisely at Al-Kiswa overlook."

"You are among family!" said my dad as he loosened his grip on the mare's lead and handed it over. "Congratulations to you!"

They shook hands. The man embraced my father, kissing his forehead, and said, "This is the most beautiful gift I have ever received in my life." He placed his hand on my father's shoulder and continued, "It is very valuable. May God give me the ability to repay you. But before it truly belongs to me, I must get to know you!"

My father replied, "Take your horse; this is not important right now. Consider it a gift from one brother to another." The man grasped my father's arm, pulling him closer. They walked several steps away, engaged in an intense conversation I could not clearly hear. Unbeknownst to me and the driver, the man secretly slipped something into my father's jacket pocket. My father resisted at first, but they eventually embraced again in a goodbye. The man gestured for his driver to take the horse's reins from my hand.

Confusion was evident on my father's face, as he did not turn toward the horse. She whinnied and pulled the driver toward us. The man told my father, "I will never forget your kindness as long as I live!" The driver led the horse away while my eyes followed them until they disappeared. Meanwhile, the man climbed into his carriage and started the engine. Waving goodbye to us, he drove toward the heart of the city.

CHAPTER FIVE

How vast is the abyss?
For those who stray from the path!

I was going to ask my father many questions about the mare's fate, but her departure left me speechless. Tears threatened to spill from my eyes. My father pulled out a handkerchief from his pocket and turned his face away. He took my hand and led me back into the market.

He carefully observed and examined the various working animals and mules. He stopped at a dark brown sturdy mule. The owner approached and, without my father asking anything, said, "It can easily pull a carriage with its load without any hassle."

"Is it experienced in plowing?" my father asked.

"No, but it is calm. You can easily train it for plowing." the man said.

"I need a tamed animal, ready for plowing," my father said.

At that moment, I was certain the blonde mare had vanished from our lives. The sturdy mule's appearance enticed me to grasp my father's hand, encouraging him to buy it. He whispered into my ear, "Buying a mule is easier than raising it." (A proverb I heard repeatedly in our village.)

I remained silent. The mule's owner failed to sway my father. Instead, my father proceeded toward another man offering a mule, though not as well-built as the first. He inquired about its availability and suitability for plowing. The man confirmed both. My father began bargaining. I paid no attention to their words. My thoughts were lost on our mare's bitter absence. Ultimately, a deal was made.

My father led me behind him, commencing the longest journey of my life. We stopped at the market by the city gate, where he bought a pound of raw coffee, cardamom seeds, oranges, cakes, sweets, and a special candy from a shop owner he knew. Again, I couldn't hear their conversation nor could I understand their hand gestures. Holding the mule's bridle while it stood as steady as a rock, I imagined our blonde mare. She was never still, flaunting and announcing a unique existence in her own space—an attribute of purebred horses that resemble humans. Now, facing a mule, its presence held no allure.

My father emerged from the shop. He placed his purchases in a saddlebag on the mule's back. On our journey, I didn't know where all the tears cascading from my eyes came from. Only two vehicles passed us on the road, just before we turned onto the dirt path leading to our village. One was a micro-bus, filled with passengers and their purchases from the city, which were carried even on its top. The other was an open carriage driven by a man wearing a foreign hat. I asked my father about the vehicles and the man.

"Those are English cars," he said, before falling silent.

"And who's driving it?" I inquired.

"Who knows!" he said, lips pinched with disgust.

My questions were an attempt to distract myself from sorrow and understand what was new and different from the village and my limited experience—or perhaps from previous lives. I noticed his reaction, though.

I wanted to ask, "What is an English car doing here?" But I choked down the question, fearing to burden my father. On that day, a change began to manifest in my father. His behavior toward my mother and everyone else became increasingly somber. He would leave for the fields with the morning star and not return until after sunset. I was cautious not to provoke his anger. That Eid Holiday, which ignited beautiful memories of the past, was what the mare, its fields, and its clouds were sold for. Yet instead of being with us, my father spent the holidays with his sister and her husband from Mount Hermon, about 50 miles away.

That Eid, our father was not among us; he who never slept on the eve of the Eid. He didn't prepare the coffee, accompanied by the sounds emanating from the minarets of the neighboring town of Dariya, their echoes reverberating through space. We didn't rise from our beds to greet him, embracing him with love and obedience. We never said to him, "May you be safe every year." He didn't say it to us or anyone else in the village.

My father disappeared for five days and then returned, but things did not revert to normalcy. The rain held back that year, causing water levels in springs and wells to drop, both in orchards and homes. The farmers harvested a meager crop insufficient for sustenance and poor-quality anise grains that wouldn't suffice even for children's needs. The leaves on trees withered in the height of summer.

One scorching summer day, my father filled a bucket with water and asked me to follow him to the yard so he could quench the mule's thirst. The mule drank gratefully, lifting its head as if to thank the heavens for this dwindling blessing. My father, growing weary of his rigid stance, patted the mule's back and sarcastically spoke as if addressing it: "Oh hero, your place is not here."

Before daylight broke the next morning, my father dressed in unusual clothes for his regular work in the wilderness. He led the mule out of our home and returned at noon without it. On another day, he sold half of our goats and stored anise seeds, causing scarcity and deterioration to become palpable.

Several young men from our village found jobs as night watchmen in the city, introducing bicycles to our community for the first time. Other young men volunteered in the national gendarmerie; including my uncle who worked for Fouad Hamza. He ended up stationed on the Syrian Jazira. For eight months, no one heard from him. Eventually, he sold his horse to repay accumulated debts and rejoined the ranks of night watchmen. He continued paying off the horse's cost from his modest monthly income.

As the villagers could not do without animals in daily life, any animal would help. I saw my father return from the city on the back of a dusty donkey one afternoon long ago. Over time, its persistent, disturbing bray began to bother us. Whereas neighing once filled my head, it was replaced by the unique braying symphonies our new guest, the donkey, entertained us with.

One of my peers shared news with me that kept me awake all night. He said, "I was grazing the goats east of the elevated hill when I saw your horse inside the fence of the Kuwaiti's farm. At first, my eyes couldn't believe what they saw. I approached the farm and confirmed it was indeed her."

He promised we would go together the following day so I could see her. As for this relative and all my neighboring peers, it is too early to talk about details of their lives, their dreams, love, and heartbreaks. However, our dusty donkey was one of the most significant losses we faced during that year's late autumn.

Throughout that night, the image of the mare and my memories with her did not leave my mind. Early in the day, with my relative, I visited the Kuwait's farm. I saw the mare inside a fence of no more than barbed wire and a row of recently planted cypress trees.

The mare was tied to a stake, which I recognized due to her circling the spot.

The mare paid attention, particularly to me. She reared up on her hind legs as if to welcome me and filled the plain with her neighing. My relative commented, "She didn't do this yesterday! Why today?"

I didn't answer but waved at her instead. She responded with louder neighs and a never-before-seen dance. She pulled on her rope until the stake dislodged and began to trot within the fence, stumbling over her rope until exhaustion took over her. She calmed down and stood facing us, visibly amazed.

A heavy tightness filled my chest, and my throat swelled with unshed tears. They started streaming down my cheeks. I wiped them away with my shirt sleeve while in shock. My vision blurred; everything seemed to spin around me. The image of a golden mare filled my head, accompanied only by the sound of her neighing within my very being. Unconsciousness overtook me, and when I woke sometime later, I found myself near Bwida canal with my relative and three shepherds he'd sought help from nearby; they'd carried me to the canal's bank. From then on, life seemed to pile upon that breaking point.

CHAPTER SIX

Don't wait for the candle to burn out
And complete your way in the darkness!

The most beautiful decision of our childhood, with youth disappearing in the fields and scattering in the square of small dreams, was to have an opportunity—in spite of the fatigue of going—to visit a neighboring village to the west. It's not because its roads, buildings, or orchards were more beautiful. It's not because its air was more pure. It's not because its water was more, fresh. It's not because its trees were more majestic. It's because everything in it greeted you with a smile. You rarely found a closed door during the day or one shut in your face. The walls of its homes were not deaf like the walls of our homes. That village intrigued me—with large windows for us to breathe through, plenty of air to enter and play in its courtyards, dancing with shrubs, grapevines, or roses.

In the fields, what attracted me were only the anise women who toiled in weeding, harvesting, and threshing. Their laughter and singing on the paths, in the fields, and in the threshing tents delighted me. Their leather headbands fascinated me, along with clothes that smelled of anise when I passed. One afternoon, my mother asked me to go with her during weeding time, to carry grass away.

"May Suha help you, my son!"

Suha was around my age and accompanied her mother to the fields for fear of being alone at home. They said their house was inhabited by jinn. Suha and I carried the grass to where the goats were and then returned. We sat on the edge of a ravine near the workers helping my mother. Suha's mother called her, "Come here, you little one. Come learn how to weed!"

Suha ran toward her mother and I followed to see. Her mother handed her the qatifa, a small sickle: "Hold it tight in your fist so it doesn't slip from your hand and cut you. You should distinguish between anise plants and grass. Coriander resembles it but coriander is considered a grass. Nothing else really looks like it. You have to uproot the grass from its roots, my daughter, or else the grass will grow back. Sit like me and crawl carefully so as not to harm the anise plant. Anise is very sensitive. Most of the grasses you will find among the anise plant are: Bermuda grass, ryegrass, coriander, chamomile, prickly holly, slender cudweed, chicory, sesbania, and oats."

Suha crossed paths unexpectedly, asking, "Will I pay attention to all this?"

Driven by curiosity, I watched the girls picking anise on the land of Al-Maliki, neighboring the row of almond trees planted next to the fence of our orchard. The girls were from a nearby village but their leader came from ours. I sat on the dry edge of the irrigation ditch, very close to them, and leaned on my elbow like an adult. Most girls stopped weeding and looked at me. The forewoman scolded them in mocking words: "This boy might kidnap one of you. Work is more important than staring at him!"

Apparently, the forewoman realized she had wronged all of us children with her harsh words. She now said, "A girl should not be tempted by anything. A girl is a gem. A gem remains a gem no matter what. A girl should weed her heart all day long and her soul all night!"

I left before the forewoman could finish her advice. The part about gems became a seed buried in my head, only to bloom later with time. However, that bloom wouldn't have been possible without Suha, who continued to work in our orchard after her mother's and my mother's death.

I learned about the stages of growing anise crops from my father and others. Anise must grow independently so no plant crowds another for nutrients, water, light, or air. Excessive density kills anise plants; they grow stronger when alone. They thrive when given space for sunlight, air, and morning dew. Anise does not accept any other plant nearby, or it will become weak. Anise doesn't accept weeding before its identity is complete, formed with at least three leaves.

Break-time. The anise workers met with the forewoman and the women in our orchard under the almond trees. They laid out the food they had brought: olives, makdous, cheese, and herbs from the ground like dandelion, thyme, and coriander; these are harmful to the anise crop.

I brought them drinking water pumped from our artesian well, usually with Suha, whenever it was my day off. We wandered on our way, taking shaded paths so no one could see us, allowing stolen moments. Like a quick embrace that lingered on me and my clothes, the scent of fatigue and anise, or a kiss that tasted like what I craved and picked from the ground—wild mint, basil, and marjoram.

Upon our return, I heard the forewoman tell Julia: "Don't do it over the anise!"

She warned Julia several times not to pee. Suha explained what Julia was doing to the anise plant after I asked. Julia told Suha that Westerners make liquor from anise, after hearing this from her brother who'd returned from working in Italy. Julia's urine would nourish the anise plant that would become their alcohol. Whoever drank it and got intoxicated would surely have to reward Julia. Perhaps God would save her from this misery. Young people dream of coral islands in far-off seas and find means to get there; but we were left in despair with no way there but to dream or resort to magic. What I do here by writing this, dear Suha, is a kind of magic like my grandmother used to say. Two days later, Suha told me the other girls secretly did the same as Julia!

Children grow up. Suha married. I continued searching for someone to fill the void she left in my soul. Days came with unexpected surprises. The charm of the liaison remained irresistible.

—

We cultivated our western field. The saying goes: "Love is a constant search for love." I fell in love again with a newfound passion. It was the brunette girl, the one who used to play with her younger brother in front of her house, the one with a short dress to her knees, a liveliness, hair torturing the air, and a swaying cross on her chest. The story of that silent and shy love faded over time.

As I pass by the place as an old man, I feel a tightness in my chest and a dryness in my throat. The memories rewind to fifty years ago. Despite this, I feel—as the implications overwhelm me—that everything is surreal. The neighboring village has become dearer to me, with its small brunette saint who refuses to grow up and its water flowing under a bridge and downhill toward my village's thirsty lands since ancient times. It waters all the flowers planted in every house, but the most beautiful one is like a kochia. There must be a reason for this.

In our family's home, there were three kochias. As the legend goes, one day during the dark times after World War I, with the French occupation of our lands after the Turkish occupation, these plants demonstrated resistance. Their defiance proved to the world that anything could resist injustice, even roses, and their fragrance. Three rebel men had hidden in the kochia bushes, and the chasing French soldiers could not discover their hiding place just two steps away.

Al-Saqiyah was supplied with water by a spring called Shawaqa. No one in the area knows why it carries this name. I created a myth about it in my head but wasn't sure if it would stand the test of time. I still recall those moments.

My relative Yahya, who learned tailoring with me in Damascus, now resides in San Francisco and holds American citizenship. When he thought about emigration, he wasn't alone in considering travel. We visited the historical town of Maaloula together and after leaving St. Mar Takla Monastery, we crossed narrow pathways that cut through mountains where St. Takla's story unfolded, in which God paved the way for her escape from evil sinners.

We reached caves dug by our Aramean ancestors as dwellings deep within ancient rocks. Sitting on a rock there, we imagined potential futures for ourselves but didn't agree on a single plan. Yahya's decision was firm, and so was mine—Yahya decided to emigrate without specifying where; more accurately, he decided to escape a painful reality only I knew about, while I stayed for reasons that would remain undisclosed even as generations passed, unless some insane hidden thoughts escaped unintentionally.

I am still immersed in the reverberations. I learned a brunette girl who worked in her father's office was from the town of Maaloula. She filled all my years of emotional drought with a single smile. Her smiles were repeated, blossoming into my adolescent poems that formed a complete collection, only lacking approval for printing and publishing. I entrusted them to my friend Jaber, who later told me they were lost when I asked for them. Both the girl who inspired these beautiful late-night writing sessions and the poems vanished with the stars, like all the other loves, disappearing into air and dust.

The reverberations open another wound, dating back to the early 1950s when I worked as a tailor in one of Damascus' ready-to-wear clothing factories. More than 50 girls worked with us—50 stars, 50 moons, 50 roses. Except for four girls who wore no veils, the others arrived in black veils and removed their wraps as soon as they entered, freeing themselves to work efficiently.

God's creations revealed their true appearance and work commenced amidst an abundance of beauty. All heights, skin colors, hair types, and everything that flows and undulates are present here. Their presence captivated teenagers like us:

Akram, Ibrahim, Taysir, and I were around 50 blossoming young girls who moved in a small space. Sewing machines took up more than half the area. We were close, surrounded by an array of fragrances that enveloped us from all directions. Each day, we raised our hands praying to the sky to bring their scorching attraction. Our hearts danced day and night whenever we received a glance or smile from any of them. Or, our hearts constricted during the day and tears washed our pillows at night if a potential love interest was seemingly uninterested or gone.

I had to navigate this forest of gazelles and avoid falling into traps set by young women planning distant marital futures. They knew that before marriage comes our military service and possibly years afterward spent securing housing and finding work with decent pay to escape a lifetime as hired laborers.

I used to call one Faten Hamama, the name of a famous actress. I imagined her weaving between sewing machines. When she arrived, each morning cloaked in black, she would bloom like the sun as she shed her layers. One day, she received a small yellow pen from me that I kept in my pocket for writing in a notebook. I kissed it while her younger sister and other girls weren't looking, and then I dropped it down her shirt as a memento.

Twenty years later, after attending Faten Hamama's movie "Duaa al Karawan" at Damascus Cinema, I still remembered that moment.

I arrived at Victoria Bridge when a woman wearing a veil approached. Suddenly, she lifted the veil off her face. She held up a small pen, the very same yellow one that had been exchanged for a lasting memory. She continued her walk, looking back just as I did. I tried to catch up with her, but she vanished like a fairy. Yes, she disappeared, leaving behind a ribbon of vivid images—a girl, tangled threads, a pen, and pain.

How numerous are the wounds and scars that lie dormant under the ashes of the years? Only to be tickled by reminiscence, becoming the masters of passing moments in fields that once blossomed with flowers. They have been withered by winds or scorched by fires.

It is impossible for anything related to emotion to die, as emotions stem from a mysterious and delicate place within the body—the heart. When its beats increase or hasten in spite of yourself, it means you'll either swim in fresh waters or drown.

The cinema introduced me to Faten Hamama, who captivated me entirely with enchantment and allure as a poor servant in "Duaa al Karawan."

She aroused my sense of manhood and jealousy, making me empathize with her, even if saving her would cost me my life. I awoke from the deception of art to see myself before a girl who resembled me as a fellow villager in her brokenness. My heroism—according to what I perceived of her—was false. Art proves to me, as acknowledged by renowned critics, that it is truer than reality.

I didn't stop there. Instead, I pondered how I could learn the address of Faten Hamama, whom the screen had painted as a servant I loved. I bought a notebook—decorated with a floral border surrounding a green heart pierced by an arrow—for writing my first love letter. I remember being cautious not to use any offensive words that might render me unworthy of her.

I didn't lie to her about anything and told her: "I am a villager's son like you." In the film, she was from a village in Upper Egypt. How naïve I was, thinking she was portraying a role that reflected her reality. I didn't tell her in the letter, "I love you," but at the end, I drew a heart like the one I had seen on the page of a cheap art magazine page carried by the wind and entangled in a thorny plant in a field unharrowed that year by its owners. Faten Hamama's address was hidden at the back of the heart's page.

I dropped my letter in the mailbox. With it, my small heart traveled the distance to the country of love. The days I waited for a reply passed heavily, as if walking with lead feet. I wasn't disappointed. The reply came, but the man who delivered mail at his store, which served as the village's post office, handed it to my father. My father became agitated and angered, scolding me with words I heard from him for the first time: "You have become a troublemaker. We will settle this at home, you lover boy. As if we need more shame in our house. We have always been decent people. You'll face consequences at home, you dog!"

After returning from the countryside, I was at home with him, face to face. He took out a large envelope from the inside pocket of his jacket, which he had folded more than once to fit within, ripping the image sent to me by her from the film "Duaa al Karawan." On the edge of the picture was a message, from which I could only read some scattered words. I gathered as much of the torn image as I could after my father threw it in my face, threatening me: "My husband Omar..... greets .....wishing you happiness.....to visit us in Egypt, and will teach you acting."

Years passed, and I never tired of following the artistic journey of Hamama. How similar I am to the hero in the story by American-Armenian writer

William Saroyan ("Dear Greta Garbo"). The boy in-fatuated with the actress Garbo chases her through a crowd of admirers, calling to her: "I would love to be an actor. I am handsome, Greta Garbo. I adore you and the art." But he disappears in the crowd and Greta Garbo never hears his voice.

—

The willow tree of life wilts, since those moments when something in the heart breaks, call it love or affir-mation of existence, or a desire for a relationship with someone of significance, rather than what transpires between lovers. Poet Ahmed Shawqi says: A glance, then a smile, then a salutation, then conversation, then an appointment, then a meeting.

To begin a new story, I entered the cinema to watch a movie. By coincidence, I had tailor's scissors that I had sharpened with an expert blacksmith. Then, in front of me sat the princess of the Rose District (I later learned her home was in the Rose District, among the moonlit houses).

Her flowing chestnut hair was in front of my eyes, cascading like a waterfall behind her seat. It command-ed me to cut a strand. My scissors conspired with me and I took a lock containing sparks that would ac-company me throughout my life, igniting their fire whenever the wind blew through the trees of my age. I followed her after the movie ended and was shocked when she closed her pink door behind her. I returned to the theater time and time again just to contemplate her image.

Thus, began a journey of concern, anxiety, and sleeplessness. Twenty years passed since I obsessed over her, laying dormant like embers beneath ashes only to awaken suddenly without warning when my heart least expected it.

My sweetheart did not appear from her pink door in the Rose District, as usual. She did not bring me a bunch of jasmines, basil, a rosebud, or a carnation. She did not show up on the balcony or in the window. No kisses flew in the air. Twenty years of absence must have changed things and altered circumstances. She must have married, moved away from the district, and possibly away from the city, too. Stubbornly, I whispered to myself: Forget the story, boy! But my attachment to her only grew stronger. She nestled within me as if part of this very moment—a sorceress.

Nature could not add an ounce of beauty. The streams could not add a ripple to her laughter. She was a full moon, transparent and pure (only her vessels and memories visible). Those who knew my story with her said: "Your love for her is a sickness."

And I bet I would never recover from it. She carried me away like a torrent and entwined me like a jinni. At the same time, I, as an earthly villager, stood before a city girl. I entered journalism for balance after self-teaching. I remained among the columns of the newspapers like an ancient statue. Poetry stole me away, and I became one who sang along with Amin Nakhl: Go sell my poem for paper money, even if it wounds history itself by this sale. Maybe through this sale, someone will dissent; paying for the trip from here to the village.

I miscalculated, thinking that my sweetheart might have been running away from a poor villager even though she lived completely above my class line. I decided to stay away from her path—damn that decision. Her pink door did not open, she did not appear. No rose, and no kiss in the air.

I didn't hear her footsteps in the hallway. Only her ghost came out of the closed pink door. I decided, for the last time, to continue searching for her. If I met her, I would tell her: I will travel and return with a fortune fitting for you. After a great effort, I did meet her. We were together, walking the path to the school where she was taking lessons to become employed. I informed her of my decision to travel for her sake and, for the first time, confessed my love. She smiled at first but then frowned. Swallowing hard, she said: You may return with a fortune, but you'll lose much love while gathering that wealth. Her footsteps shook the sidewalk but she never turned toward me. That old image of her appears in my mind, still wearing the school uniform proudly. Her ghost vanishes; the door remains closed.

A cold breeze blows and the rustling leaves of trees standing like guards on either side of the street fall. The yellow leaves are guided by the wind toward lifeless corners. In my pocket is her first and last letter to me; I can recite it word for word without unfolding it. The last line says: "I will not live with a selfish husband beneath a sky where I can only see as far as our bed." Basically, I won't settle for a bathtub imagining it as an ocean.

Twenty years passed. I do not know what magical force led me to the Rose district, as I still do not know what magical force made my boyhood self sneak a jasmine flower into her red coat pocket, the one she wore over her school uniform on cold days.

In those moments, a bulldozer crossed the neighborhood. Its tracks crushed one of the houses, mixing soil with hibiscus, jasmine, Damask roses, dandelion greens, and the soul's herbs. Will the eyes of construction traders overlook my girl's house? Will they leave it as a memory? Will they see beauty as the moon peering from a door or the sun shining through a porch lattice?

The sound of footsteps in the hallway, on the stairs, or the walls that protected my girl's face from dust. The orange tree that was delighted by her humming and laughter. If only the bulldozer could remove the petrified lump in my throat.

I noticed a man dusting off his modest storefront. I peered behind it to see drawings: enlarged pictures of people, covered pictures—perhaps to preserve secrets or protect them from dust. I wondered to myself: Why not enlarge my girl's picture? He greeted me suspiciously while examining my face: Are you one of those who buys old houses in this neighborhood and demolishes them? I reassured him that I had nothing to do with that and declared my annoyance about random demolition of heritage-worthy houses. He welcomed me and asked what I sought by entering his store. I said, "I have a photo I want to enlarge."

As soon as he saw her in my hand, he snatched it. He screamed, "She resembles my daughter!" And then screamed again while staring at it intensely and trembling. "It's her! It's her, indeed!"

There was nothing to do but flee. I never walked through the neighborhood again, even though I later worked nearby and believed my story with the neighborhood was forever buried.

CHAPTER SEVEN

**Sex in impoverished societies
only to fill a void in the soul, time, or love!**

A Mexican magician said to his apprentice: "Every time you look at something, its shape changes. If you manage to focus on everything, there will be no difference between what you do when you dream and what you do when you sleep!"

In our childhood, we play as temporary creatures to stay alive, to ensure that we are alive. That we will grow up and do as our predecessors did. We repeat the same actions, their successes, and their mistakes.

Myself and Afifa, who pretended to be ill so she wouldn't have to go with her working mother to harvest anise. For the first time, we were alone in the house—it had always been buzzing like a beehive. My father and uncle shared everything: the house, farming, cattle, and bread-making. They even divided ownership of land and worked on a sharecropping basis.

Today will be her day, while I am a stranger unaware of everything she had prepared. The lives of the deprived, oppressed, and the downtrodden in closed and miserable societies—even the pleasures of food and all necessities are summoned; everything oppressive has a secret path!

"Let's play hide and seek, Afifa!" I said.

She removed her headscarf and blindfolded me.

"Face the wall. Don't remove the blindfold until I shout 'Ready!'" she said.

With no other choice, I, the young Adam, was assigned by the blossoming Eve to search. Her footsteps echoed lightly and faded. After a moment, her voice came from a distance:

"Ready!"

I freed my eyes from Afifa's blindfold and tossed it toward a bushy pomegranate tree in the courtyard. I tried to pinpoint the source of her voice but failed.

I set off. She was not behind the haystacks, nor among the storage shelves in the provisions room as I expected. She didn't hide among one of the three kochia bushes that a great-aunt from Mount Harmon had planted; she had come as the "fiancée" of a young man from that mountain. They were both newcomers. The young man stayed in the guest room, and she stayed in the women's room. Two weeks later, the village elder approved their marriage. After, they moved into a separate room together. That night, they closed and locked their door.

One time, I pushed open their door to enter but my father scolded me when he noticed. I asked my aunt what they were doing. She scolded me.

"It's a shame!" she said.

They lived in our house a long time, helping with various chores without being asked.

—

At first, my attempts to find Afifa were fruitless. I tried the cattle barn, the stable, and the abandoned ruins in the yard. She was not supposed to hide in any of the rooms. I stopped, straining to hear anxiously. My gaze fell upon the well in the center of the courtyard—suddenly it occurred to me: God forbid that! But I did not hear any commotion or cry from the direction of the well. Still, I approached it cautiously and threw a stone into it. Only the sound of the stone reverberated from the well. What should I tell people? I shouted: "Afifa-a!" No one answered.

The beehive was empty but for Afifa who remained indoors guarded by our home. I yelled again: Afifaaa! No one answered. I heard a broken meow, far away, and from above. It was revealed. She must be in the haystack in the barn. My sorrow turned into overwhelming joy. The haystack is full, only about a yard from the barn's ceiling. Could Afifa have risked hiding in it? She must be there; it's the only place not searched. I climbed a wooden ladder leading to the loft. The door, which she had closed and propped by a dead apricot tree trunk, remained exactly as it was. When I peeped through a window to the haystack, Afifa laughed out loud, lying on top of the hay's surface high up. To win the game you had to touch and not merely see. I had to touch Afifa. I jumped through the window into the heart of the haystack. The rank of stored hay choked me. I touched Afifa with my fingertip.

She grabbed me by the shoulder. The hay was soft under my feet. I fell to lie down. The smell of the hay intensified, causing me more discomfort. Afifa's arm encircled me. Her eyes and voice pleaded:

"Let's sleep a little, then we get out of here. Sleep now, and I'll play another beautiful game with you when we leave."

"What is it?" I asked.

"Let it be a surprise," she said.

She tightened her coiled arm around my neck. Her leg pressed firmly against mine. I couldn't escape, as a fly caught in a spider's web. She brushed off some hay that had stuck to my hair. Her eyes sparkled, looking at me as if she wanted to say something. Hesitating and cautious, she said, "Close your eyes. There is dust on your face; I will remove it."

I closed my eyes. Her fingers moved back and forth on the skin of my face, with the gentle rustle of butterfly wings. She kissed my cheek and pressed her mouth to mine until I almost suffocated. I tried to pull away, expressing my displeasure to her but she lowered her gaze in modesty. I told her, "There are many rooms in the house. I won't sleep on hay."

"Sleeping on hay is better than sleeping on a woolen mattress," she said, clearly agitated.

She hugged me tighter. Her dress receded, revealing floral underpants. Star-shaped patterns intermingled with the flowers. Rows of ruffles adorned the legs. The zigzag of tassels. They were covered by straw, hiding the colors within the fabric of her underpants that radiated warmth.

Her unreasonable thoughts:

"Let's hide together, with an imaginary child searching for us, on the condition that we're in the pantry... No. In the barn... No. In the well... No. In the broom closet... No."

She brought a mat from the winter room to the courtyard.

"This place is safe! An exposed location dispels suspicion. Yes. Let's go. Here, they cannot see us! They won't expect us to hide here. We won't play with a child who would find us instantly; we won't entertain one so clever and cunning. Here we'll stay until evening, unseen by anyone."

"Let's play another game," I said.

"'The Bath.' Come on, let me bathe you!" she said.

"How? Without any washcloths or soap?"

"It's just a game!"

Afifa washed my hair, face, and neck before drying me off—then my chest and waist.

"Your turn is over; let's continue playing elsewhere!" she said.

"Where?" I said.

"In one of the rooms. I always bathe with a basin placed in front of a room's door while I close myself inside." Her gaze urges me to hurry.

"My lovely companion always rubs my back. This time, it's your turn," she said.

"I'll make the blood flow from your back, Afifa!"I said.

Marble columns stand at the threshold. A green mulberry leaf, from two crossed palms, dances on the water.

Is it a navel? No, it is an abandoned chamomile flower, amid dew and snow. Afifa shivers.

"You're shivering, Afifa!" I said.

"The water is cold, as are your fingers," she said.

Afifa lies down.

"Rub my back," she said.

My childhood rubs Afifa's back. Climbing slopes and hills. Afifa turns over. My childhood returns to Afifa, rubbing her chest and offering her comfort. She embraces me.

"I am your lover. Sleep with me. I am your lover. Learn," she said.

Not long after, when I helped the girls lift Afifa onto the mare on her wedding night, my cousin Ayyoub and I left the children's dance circle and caught up with Afifa, the bride. The night was adorned with Afifa.

A sugar-colored dress. Shimmering beads glistened in the candlelight. A silky veil like a piece of white cloud. A wreath upon her high forehead. A queen without subjects. A princess without a land. The mare was recently tamed. Blonde and bridled. A white marking between her eyes. The taller girls guarded Afifa against falling off the playful horse with an impromptu dance. The groom's attendant held the reins tightly at the nearest point to the bridle.

CHAPTER EIGHT

**It is not easy to uproot a tree
laden with fruit and transplant it to
another location,
even if it were in its original habitat.**

I do not know what attracted Afifa to work for my family during the anise seasons, despite the passing of three thin and scarce seasons. I told her about my grandfather, Mustafa, and how my mother cries for him whenever he is mentioned in her presence, although she does not know him at all. He traveled immediately after her birth. We were alone in the anise-pounding tent when she asked me about my elusive grandfather:

"I saw him, Afifa. I saw him returning to his homeland, but in a dream. He waved his handkerchief, soaked with tears, to the last point of Latin America as he bid it farewell after half a century in exile.

My grandfather came back a few days after my dream, leaving behind many memories, dreams, and children. He said goodbye to the land of yerba mate, carnivals, and rebels and returned here—to a circular movement in time—like a lost blazing star returning to its orbit in his village and putting down his luggage. The villagers gathered to receive him; their heads, which knew nothing on the world map beyond the boundaries of their village and what bordered it, held only naive thoughts about this man overflowing with life from different places, women, and experiences.

One of them said, "Discard this hat, Sheikh Mustafa. The turban is more fitting for an older man's head like yours. You are now the elder of your family; you are the oldest among them."

My grandfather cleared his throat and said, "I may not stay long."

"We will not let you leave the village," said a villager.

Then murmurs arose among those present along with whispers and soft one-on-one conversations that echoed in his hearing as he cringed.

"No doubt he married someone from there—a foreigner—and has a family with her. Who knows?"

"He might be unable to stay away from his wife— he can't live without a woman!"

"We could have him marry one here."

"He may miss his wife in Argentina."

"A woman for a woman!"

"And may she be the loveliest girl."

My grandfather was yielding to these comments and flitting opinions. Sarcasm surged within him as he said, "What beautiful things you all say."

One person noticed his sarcasm and, pressing his lips together, hummed, "Of course, 'money brings the loveliest bride!'"

Another noticed my grandfather's unease and said, "Gentlemen, please stop this talk. Ask Uncle Mustafa to speak to us about that country."

A man sitting opposite countered, "What concern do we have with that country? It offers us no benefit. Since we're unfamiliar with it and will never visit, let him discuss more important matters: his work, the wealth he accumulated during his long exile."

My grandfather replied with a forced smile, "Those are appropriate questions."

The man insisted, "Well then, share with us."

Grandfather said, "I worked as a farmer like my father. Accumulating wealth was not my purpose while abroad."

The chief of the largest family remarked arrogantly, "Others managed to bring money in large bags."

"As for me, I didn't migrate for that purpose, and money didn't concern me. It's enough that I lived, got married, and had children like you, and was extremely happy. More than that; I explored a new country."

My grandfather heard one of them whisper in the ear of the man sitting next to him mockingly: "Cats know how to get married! The man returned penniless. That's the whole story!"

Others irritated him. He shifted his gaze towards them. He read the secrets of their eyes and their hearts. He said to himself, "Curse them. As if the earth hasn't turned during my absence." Everyone moved away from his chest, burdened with the wounds of estrangement, filled with the air of distant lands, charged with ashes from years spent away from his birthplace, childhood dream circle, and youth, still containing glowing embers or remnants.

And, now, he stood face-to-face before his first son, my uncle, and a stream of bitter reproach. My grandfather tried his best to tell his son what was once at stake for males in their village, family, friends, and himself.

"My son, the road was blocked. We had no choice but to take to the sea and flee like teardrops from an eye.

We endured the oppression of the Ottoman, but not our war, which was neither our concern nor responsibility. I told Hamed and Khalil, who were ordered by the governor to join the conscription army, immediately: 'We shall not be like lambs. We will not allow them to lead us to our death willingly. Let's find a quick solution, even though it means leaving you behind.'"

"And no news, no updates, you oppressor!" said my uncle. "As if you don't have a wife and children here. Who could convince me that you're my father? I do not know your face or your voice. I don't know the warmth of your palms. I never slept a night on your arm. But blood does not turn into water."

"My son, consider the hardship of my return and take pity on my age. My coming back here means returning to you, your sister, our family. I came back to speak with people in my language as I did when I was a child and a young man. To this village, that I know better than all of you. I can describe every aspect of it—even the air that passes through its orchards, its paths, its alleys, its streets, and the sounds of its springs. This body of yours—I bathed it in tears on the night we parted."

My grandfather threw himself upon his uncle's chest sobbing. Uncle wiped away his tears with his fingers and said: "Take comfort; blood doesn't turn into water. You are here among us. We will protect you from harm at any cost. Tomorrow morning when the sun rises we will visit the places where you grew up and loved. Do you remember those places?"

"Yes, my son. They always appeared before my eyes as creatures with souls. My son, can you tell me about your mother Badura? My conscience torments me because of her since I left the country."

"She got married—due to the lack of news from you—and gave birth to a loving brother and sister for us. Remember the first man who kissed your cheeks and was your first guest to welcome you back? It is him."

"The poor woman; I wronged her."

"I will let you go now to bed. Take care of yourself. The change in the atmosphere might affect you."

My grandfather's pillow became soaked with tears; it is not easy to uproot a tree laden with fruits, even to plant it back in its original homeland, in its very original soil. Memories were attacking his mind like flocks of thirsty birds encountering water. His inner voice was stronger than sleep itself. He spoke to his wife in Argentina.

"Maria, forgive me; for I'm moving away from your resting place. From now on, I won't visit your grave on birthdays to gift you a bouquet of flowers. How many nights did I tell you stories about Antarah, Al-Muhallhal, Zir Salem, Al-Zainati, Jassas, Kulaib and so much more until we were full? You got me used to being honest with you, so I revealed everything to you. I told you that I'm already married and have a son and a daughter in my home country. You didn't get angry; instead, your anger focused on me when I told you that I knew nothing about them."

"Why don't you write to them? I don't know you, devoid of feelings," you said.

"I don't know how to write," I replied.

"But I see you reading?"

"I never learned how to write!"

"Come on, find an Arab from your people who can write."

You angrily said when I didn't answer:

"You should have learned."

Then you got up, brought a book from my books that I carried with me here. You opened it. You moved your gaze between its lines. Your finger nervously traced the words until it almost pierced the paper, before saying:

"Look. This character is like this one, and that is like this one."

Then you slammed the book on my face angrily and said, "Just like you learned how to read, learn how to write. Get up. Get up. And I will hold your fingers to draw the letters."

"Ah, Maria. How did you agree to live with me no matter what? How happy we were, Maria. You taught me the language of that country, and I taught you how to cultivate the fallow land. You taught me how to wake up smiling, and I taught you how to open the water wheel for irrigation of thirsty plants. Alone among farmers, in one season, I got a pair of oxen. Oh, Maria! I never knew I would need writing. One man wrote for all the villagers."

You said: "You are not a fish that doesn't leave water! Didn't you know that you would travel?"

I lied to her and said: "No. I was traveling in a dream, and how I wished it to be true. I was sitting under a tree. I closed my eyes, dreaming and visiting countries, rivers, mountains, and plains in the dream, women, sailing boats fighting waves. And why not travel, Maria? The genie made a lamp for Aladdin in order for him to reach any place on Earth. I imagined that in countries, seas, and distant islands one would find women of indescribable, transcendent beauty. The further the journey, the more beautiful were the women. And things were more beautiful as the pearls for the divers were the most beautiful and rare in the depths. As experienced sailors have sea brides with green eyes like forests or blue-like horizons. Voices with nothing more creative than their chimes. Bodies glowing like rainbows."

"And what about women in your hometown, Mustafa?" she said.

I still remember this difficult question. With bitterness, I answered that day: "They give birth like cats. They work with us like mules. Their veins are prominent in their necks, the cracks deep on their feet!"

You interrupted me then angrily: "And here I am working like an animal. Responding to your desires in giving birth. It won't be long before I turn into an image of them."

"You're different, Maria. You're warm."

You told me without conviction: "Perhaps! The body only generates warmth as much as it takes. Even the sun cools down in winter." I touched your hair and chest, and after that, you said confidently: "I don't think I'm different from your women, Mustafa! Tell me your opinion of your wife, Badura, whom you left to her fate. Tell me how you met her. Be careful not to lie to me. I know a person when they lie!"

"I didn't tell you the truth, Maria. Badura is not a stranger to me. She is my cousin. She was the most beautiful girl. The scent of anise, which emanated from her when she passed by, still fills my chest. I only met her during the anise seasons—during its weeding and harvesting."

"I wronged you, my cousin. If only the days could return. If only time could rewind so I could hear your voice, laughter, and sweet jokes again."

That day, a new morning dawned on this aged grandfather like vintage wine. He couldn't believe he was in his beloved yet harsh village. My uncle went with him to the place he had designated – the location of the olive press.

"I want to see it," he said without revealing that his mother, Badura's hook was embedded in his heart there, becoming his wife one day. He remembered those rivulets overflowing with plants—the flowers he loved, their scent intoxicating. The nights spent in the anise tent threshing it out and those swarms of girls passing by heading to nearby fields along Bu Louis canal and the bridge. Badura's grandmother's spirit appeared; he averted his face from my uncle with un-intended sadness in his eyes. Uncle noticed him and said: "Let's go back home, Father."

My grandfather, while inspecting what he had seen half a century ago, told my uncle with a voice of overflowing sadness: "No trees or greenery as in the past, my son! Let's go back home."

CHAPTER NINE

Two Hopeless Men:
A man who does not love,
And a man not loved.

Every evening, I returned from work on my bicycle, weighed down with nostalgia for a village whose biological clock was perfectly in sync with its time loop.

In this village, all the people share one truth: they live a lifestyle they fully understand; they rise with the dawn, disperse into fields and orchards, return in the evening, and stay up by moonlight, lantern, or oil-lamp light; they eat whatever food is available and sleep like the dead due to fatigue.

The husbands have a way to release their emotions of anger, oppression, or misery; their wives. Their wives certainly transform these emotions into procreation, which nature recommends and men take pride in. Husbands assert themselves upon their wives, who possess no power to say "no," resist, refuse, defy, or escape. Instead of retaliation, these women submit as a form of revenge—inflicting more harm on their husbands whom they've deemed aggressive since falling into their beds and losing their dreams of being swept away by a prince on a white horse or even an old donkey. But rather than that fate, they are led hand-in-hand on an unforgettable night behind elders and clergymen who recite the same verses chanted during funerals.

I was still in my early youth, and my concern was how to break free from the familiar and shatter the rules. A teenager like me finds himself alone at night, haunted by fantasies and thoughts that cannot be pushed away. These fantasies are often close to reality or similar.

One night, I wasn't feeling well; during the day, while in the city, I waited for Khalida, a girl I worked with, to go to the cinema for an Indian film. The film had been playing for two months, telling a love story between a poor boy and a rich girl. Fate played its part in bringing them together, and they got married after a long journey of suffering that led to happiness. This movie served as a dose of intoxication for impover-ished youth, fueling our hopes.

But Khalida didn't show up, leaving me with the choice to either watch the movie alone for the fifth time or leave. However, the fragility of a country boy like me in the city kept hope alive. Khalida would either come or not come. Still, this delicate young man was prone to ponder and dream until the end of time.

Khalida never came to meet me. I, the villager, discovered that Khalida—who also had the right to dream—was smitten by a wealthy boy. Instead, she agreed to watch the same film at the screening after the one I saw. When I left, seeing her laugh with that boy—a picture of elegance in ironed clothes and shiny black shoes—provided a stark contrast to my appearance, clothes wrinkled because of my bike ride from the village to the city. My proposed romantic rendezvous earned me no kiss or even tough, only a glance and sigh.

I knew her voice well. The subjects of our conversations would never stray beyond sewing or talking about other girls at our workplace. I didn't let her see me at the cinema, nor did I reprimand her at work. I didn't cloud her dreams. Our emotional connections did not involve religious beliefs or the possible consequences if they were to evolve beyond innocent encounters.

Calculations differ when waking from a fantastical idea, and the balance indicator stands at its limit. I return to myself and bitterly ask with pain: Why didn't

I pay attention to my rural rose, Suha? That jug on her shoulder was filled with clouds and heaven's water, while she walked like a graceful gazelle between the water source and home. Even when she had a house and children were born, she remained the woman my imagination had created to be the first link in an endless chain lost between reality and dream, between substance and illusion—reduced from thousands of women—even that gypsy who danced during festivals and celebrations.

The sparkle in Suha's eyes touched the heart. Her soul's flute resounded, and her necklace beads transformed into stars. The stars became colorful butterflies, dancing through the void. Her voice rang like a hive of bees in his head, breaking free toward the meadows. Wrapped in a small world, she was led down a short path and into an arranged marriage; each new day bringing fields, a village, family, neighbors, and laughter. For her, the village remained the edge of the world.

Fatima, who was also my companion, walked behind me on the way to the mill, us both with heavy loads on our backs.

"Can you help me keep my load steady while crossing the canal?" she asked.

"I'm here for you," I said.

A stray donkey charged toward us but stopped briefly to challenge us with a neigh before carrying on. Fatima's donkey was startled and dropped everything. With our arms around each other, we lifted the fallen sack together. My grip tightened on her wrist; she winced in pain—an exclamation forever etched in my memory.

The scent of Fatima's hands tinged with anise lingered on my knapsack to the city. That knapsack was stolen by the city and passed from Fatima onto Sawsan, my coworker, at the silent sewing machines. Images of the enticing Sawsan repeated every day: a plastic rose on her chest; a red ribbon in her hair; an innocent face; eyes that broke the monotony. The plastic rose became perfume; the red ribbon flashed like lightning; stars radiated in her hair matching the stars in the sky—a full moon emerged nightly as reality gave way to dreams.

Rainbows arched before Sawsan as she crossed streets above clouds and fog, every entrance to work shadowed by a multicolored bridge. The sun clung to her window throughout working hours until it followed her home—fields of violets in tow. Moons descended, settling like a crown upon her brow to guard her through the night. From her cheeks down to the first button of her blouse, it bathed her in its warm glow.

Just as fast, the city stole the stars and moon from Sawsan's hair and the sun returned to the heavens. Rainbows vanished and the bridge collapsed. A man stood in Sawsan's fate, like a wall—possessing all the qualities of charm and marriage. I would straighten and iron collars for Sawsan while she sewed them. Eventually, I took on both tasks so that Sawsan could continue to weave her waking dreams.

A persistent nightmare loomed over my happiness, one that cannot be dispelled, eventually killing all joy. I leave the tailor's workshop defeated and retreat from the world that temptation has stolen. In my defeat, I found solace in the shadows of the anise-threshing tent and reading books.

What did I do when the heroes of novels win the women in books or when the author himself does? Why can't I have what they have? From now on, no girl shall ever be stolen from my papers by the protagonist. My first heroine was Bouhaird, when she visited the Golan Heights in Syria, where I served in the military. I waved to her as she stood tall like a palm tree, riding in an open military vehicle. My story with her was lost in the Six-Day War.

Second, there was May Ziade, whom Gibran Khalil Gibran loved before me. He left me nothing from her but what he left for the admirers of her literary salon and the mental hospital that took her away in its nights. Resentments and greed were inherited by those who coveted everything she had, except for what she penned for us with the ink of her soul.

The third, fourth, fifth, hundredth, and thousandth—all just pictures of my imagination. They were dreamers like me who searched for love afar but overlooked that it existed closer than the blood running through their jugular veins. Sightless to what lay in front of them, they focused on distant illusions.

How close were the daughters of anise. Before the village spring and its streams dried up, they were like stars walking on Earth. Strings of pearls upon the village's chest. Their images dissipated in my distant and unattainable dreams, in the verdant fields, on the paths infused with their essence, never parting from the scent of the soil. Along the banks of streams, under the shadows of willows, jujubes, and almond trees. At weddings, and in the mystery of death, when one of their hearts leaped from its cage to soar in the vastness of love.

The cycle of life turned them into falling meteors, extinguishing in the process. They were not born for this fate. They never knew they were the pulse at the heart of existence—the journey of the circulatory cycle to the body of survival, continuity, and expansion. It was in their care to nurture greenery, watch over hope, light, water calls, starry gleams, and night sounds.

Within their realm, they made heads spin and infused joy with delight, and delight with love. They produced a different kind of love unlike that which Earth produces from grains to stave off hunger.

Anise seeds are produced, but they don't know they dispelled another hunger, after becoming alcohol. This hunger is called worry, sadness, or depression. Here, anise has no use other than being boiled like tea and consumed as a remedy for headaches or stomach cramps.

My grandmother was restless in the anise-threshing tent on her last day of work, alongside young girls, like herself grumbling about something unknown to me. I dared and asked her the reason. Suha winked, implying that my angry grandmother wouldn't answer.

After work ended and the girls left the tent, my grandmother called to me. She requested that

I sit on a heap of anise straw in front of her. As I sat down, she said:

"You asked me, my son. I didn't want to talk in front of the girls, so they wouldn't despise their lives. Each one of us works tirelessly all year like a beast of burden just to acquire one garment to ward off the cold. We still don't know why anise is planted in this country. They say that they make a drink from it that causes people to lose their minds. I tried many times to boil and drink it, but nothing happened. Once, I wished to lose my mind too. I longed to drink what they create from this anise and never wake up until the anise season was over!"

And later after that confession, her spirit embraced heaven before she could even taste or know the name of such a drink—Arak.

When I grew older, I came to understand the tale of the anise and its dimensions—this remarkable plant. I became familiar with the seed, I learned the farmer, merchant, middleman, shipping vessels, and distant lands distilled it and returned it to us. I realized that every drop of anise was equated with a handful of tears, a handful of sweat resulting from labor, much joy, dreams, riddles, laughter, and bitter weddings.

I learned that anise is alive while Arak is merely a calculation.

Anise has its expanse while Arak stays in cellars. Anise's girls are destined to be born in light and air and ultimately end up in a bottle, so is Anise.

The cultivation of anise in our village has all but ceased. No merchant came to bemoan our village's fate or lament our loss, for they knew where and how to find what they sought. And because time never repeats the same moments, I am left with only memories, from which I craft a metaphorical Arak, making me regret nothing at all.

CHAPTER TEN

The silkworm
doesn't care
who would wear its silk!

Every evening, I return from work on my bicycle, weighed down with longing for a village that has a biological clock that is perfectly in sync with looping time. In this village, all the people share one truth: they live a lifestyle that they fully understand and are used to. They rise with the dawn, disperse into fields and orchards, return in the evening, and gather by moonlight, lantern, or oil-lamp light. They eat whatever food is available and sleep like the dead due to fatigue.

The husbands have a way to release their emotions of anger, oppression, or misery; their wives. Their wives certainly transform these emotions into procreation, which nature recommends and men take pride in. Husbands assert themselves upon their wives, who possess no power to say "no," resist, refuse, defy, or escape. Instead of retaliation, these women submit as a form of revenge—inflicting more harm on their husbands whom they've deemed aggressive since falling into their beds and losing their dreams of being swept away by a prince on a white horse or even on a lame donkey. But rather than that dream, they are led hand and hand on an unforgettable event behind elders and clergymen who recite the same verses that are chanted during funerals.

Oh memory, to which forgetfulness does not come close when it comes to loss.

When I returned from work on that sorrowful evening, I found my ailing mother clinging to the iron window bar in the room she'd entered as a bride and lived in since her wedding day, once a golden cage. Her wedding dress was now cast aside and stained with the mud of a time whose heavy footsteps still echo throughout the universe. She gasped due to a suffocating asthma attack, in pain. I felt helpless, unable to alleviate her suffering. Our neighbor left and brought back the Bedouin woman, Um Aqeel, from her tent, hoping she could treat my mother. We couldn't get other medical help due to the lack of transportation to the city at that time.

I left my mother's room and exited it to dwell among the stars. Azrael, the Angel of Death, continued to snatch the souls of women who had suffered from exhaustion, oppression, and rape within marriage without mercy. Azrael returned at the same time the following year to take my little sister where our mother resides, after being consumed by typhoid fever for sixty days.

After a few years, it was my brother Yusuf, that earthly angel who had been one with the fields, its soil, irrigation channels, trees, almond blossoms, and anise. He too had to leave this world in the prime of his youth when his liver suffered an incurable ailment, despite the best care available.

What pained me more than bidding him farewell was my trip with family members to retrieve his body from the morgue of the hospital where he had passed away. His body lay haphazardly on the morgue's floor, resembling a victim abandoned. My heart clenched. It is difficult to describe those painful moments. I wished his soul could find solace in departing this world, reborn in a place that respects both the living and dead, with a family deserving of this kind angel who never had a mother's loving nurture. Since he was a little boy, female relatives took turns visiting our home to raise him after our mother died.

My grief for his death deepened when I saw that watch—the one I gifted him on his wedding day—shining on the wrist of the morgue keeper.

My brother's shadow chases me, and I feel his absence because I couldn't provide him anything to ward off the specter of poverty, even for a moment. His heart pulled him by his hair, just as my heart pulled me into the world of writing.

So many times, I have failed to write an elegy for those we have lost despite their love for life. They left without harming any creature. They departed only with their white shrouds soaked in the rain of our tears or our souls, or whatever you choose to call it. I repeatedly express my desire to write, yet words betray me. Perhaps this is because writing is not born from desires. I ask myself: Do demons or angels gather in the writer's head when they sit at the writing table? Or do they take turns? I pondered this riddle deeply.

Moon (an Arabic saying for a beautiful woman) after moon fades in a village where only the sad beats of its heart can be heard. In contrast, numerous influential heads in the village do not even deserve a haircut, those heads never thought that life, as it evolves, may also fade. However, human errors do not stop at people such as this.

Some stories look pale compared to what happened to the young goat-herder, Marae. His story spread around the village and became a source of entertainment, but always told secretly.

Like hemp in the wind, Marae trembled in the presence of Sheikh Wakid when he returned early with the thirsty goats, one day, because the water of Bardi Pond was dusty and muddy due to the harvest work and drought that year. The irrigation water stopped flowing. The Sheikh punched him and yelled, "Bring hay for the animals!" The Sheikh's harsh words were harder than the work itself and more painful than the dry dust of the threshed anise in the eye. Marae's only consolation in work was that Muzna accompanied him on his daily journey from anise fields to their home.

"Your face is dusty, Muzna!" he said.

"We're late, move faster, Marae," she said.

"I was thinking of leaving the village."

"Leaving the village?"

Muzna tried to hide her surprise, but noticed the defeat in his eyes and looked away. Marae hesitated, then regained his composure, masking his unease.

"But I changed my mind, Muzna. As I lay my head on the pillow, the village's issues invaded my thoughts, just like this herd of goats digging through the dirt in search of living roots."

"The village issues, Marae?"

"Oh, yes, Muzna. Every wall we leaned on had

a unique charm to it that nourished our souls. Each stone we sat on provided a lingering warmth that flowed through us. The trees, the waterways, the plows, the axes, and the sickles."

"And what about your people, Marae?"

"Forget about the people."

"And what about me?"

Marae smiled warmly. Muzna returned his smile shyly.

"Do you remember when we were children, running around the women weeding in the anise fields and chasing butterflies? I used to pick flowers and weave them into your hair."

"I remember."

"And when the canal guard caught us at Khuder's shrine during the festival of Holly Thursday?"

She pretended not to remember that day when they were stopped by the guard before their supposed first kiss.

"No, I don't remember."

He reminded her.

"That game that never got played. If only we could play it throughout our lives like the rest of creation. Muzna, even the terrifying events in our village had another taste in our hearts. My father dreamed of being human and was killed because he raised his voice for justice. He didn't even own a piece of land. Even, my uncle whose mind was stolen by jinn at the abandoned mill."

"No, your uncle had a wild imagination, Marae!"

"No, Muzna. His problem was that he stumbled upon a goat which started following him while he was riding his donkey. Then, he noticed the goat quickly grew in size and began digging the earth with its hooves. He had been struck with insanity, and lived his final days out of his mind."

"I don't believe these tales of jinn!"

"Um Ali, heard the sound of a drum in her house, a jinn singing, and the rhythm of a wild dance. Hamdo also, after being locked up by the landlord in a chicken coop. They said, 'The jinn stole his mind.'"

"I never heard Um Ali's story!"

"I'm not lying, Muzna. When Um Ali heard the noise of the jinn, she was terrified and started wailing. The neighbors rushed to her house—Um Mohamed, her daughters, and her son. They splashed water on Um Ali's face. When she opened her eyes and looked around anxiously, she asked them: 'What are you doing? Where am I?'

"At that moment, Um Mohamed answered her, alleviating the horror of what she had witnessed: 'You are in our hearts. Tell us what happened?'

"Um Ali replied that she had heard the beating of a drum and singing unlike anything she had ever heard before, along with the rhythm of dancing coming from her house, even though the doors were closed. 'Jinn inhabits our house!' Um Ali said.

"Um Mohamed tried to calm her down: 'I don't think so; you're just imagining it, Um Ali. Let's enter the house together so I can prove it to you!'"

Marae continued attempting to refute her disbelief.

"Your mother told me that you were with her when you entered the storeroom one day and saw flour, bulgur, lentils, and raisins scattered all around. You also saw embers still glowing in the hearth of the indoor winter room. The dishes had leftovers in them. The house is haunted. It is inhabited by Jinn!"

"That's what they say, but I don't believe it," Muzna said.

"Are you accusing your mother?"

"That's not what I meant."

"Will I see you tomorrow, Muzna?"

"No!"

"What?"

"People have started talking about us, Marae. Oh, you remember the girl from the Krayem family who was killed, her blood hasn't dried yet!"

Sheikh Wakid shouted from outside the hut.

"Marae, feed the bulls!"

Marae's hands scooped the hay and mixed it with grass, while a nearby bull tried to charge at him. He remembered that Um Asharaf had told him one day: "In this hayloft, a jinn bride emerges during the Feast of the Cross, wails, and vanishes when someone appears."

Suddenly, a rope slipped onto Marae's foot. Distracted by the jinn story and filled with fear, he threw the forage in front of him and ran away terrified.

In another encounter with Muzna, while she was returning from harvesting anise, he told her what had happened in the barn.

"I didn't see the bride of jinn, Muzna; I only heard a groan," he said.

"You're crazy."

"Your heart is pure."

"You see me this way because you have not yet entered my heart."

Muzna lifted her leather forehead cover. She wiped the harvest dust from her forehead with her sleeve. Her gaze settled on Marae's face. She smiled, and he returned the smile.

"Your voice is filled with sadness," he said.

"Sheikh ... wants me as his wife."

Marae's head started to burn like reeds on fire. The river left its two banks. Pomegranate blossoms wilted. The sun wove its rays into a necklace of flames around his neck. Steps stole the dirt paths, and thorns wounded the butterflies.

"The Sheikh is hoping for the impossible, Muzna."

"I heard him saying, 'If I cannot have her because of my age, then my son must have her.'

"And as long as I live, no!"

"The eye can't stop the drill, Marae. You'll find someone better and more beautiful than me."

"You're saying this, Muzna?"

"Because I'm scared for you."

"If you keep thinking like this, you won't see my face again after today."

He paused. "I'll leave this village and go away."

"Where will you go?"

"The world is vast."

Marae's journey led him to Beirut. He didn't stay long before news of him faded completely. Years later, news resurfaced in Argentina. There, he avoided meeting emigrants from his village. My grandfather, Mustafa, told Marae's relatives about him when they asked during his visit from Argentina.

"I saw him once, then he disappeared entirely. Many theories surround his disappearance. It's likely that he died; but it wasn't an ordinary death. They say he was killed because of a woman. Only God knows!"

It comes as no surprise that such tragedies ignite fires, only to be extinguished and followed by caution to prevent recurrence. However, what's astonishing is that these fires keep happening time and time again, as if nothing had happened.

Life starts anew. If we are destined to remain alive, we will watch, listen, read, imagine, and anticipate many stories cut short before completion. Countless lives, however, follow a path similar to the winter moon, often obscured by clouds so we cannot see its entire trajectory. Likewise, the stories of many people are obscured and cut short before their proper ending.

CHAPTER ELEVEN

Just as love is a lifestyle,
hatred is also a lifestyle.

Disappointment stories dominated people's gatherings. We were just boys, obliged to listen. We couldn't talk in the presence of adults, and we stored whatever we heard in our memories without control. After a night of conversations and tales about jinn, demons, suffering in the grave, and the hereafter, I couldn't sleep due to the anxiety that gripped me and the nightmares that might invade if I dozed off.

The following night marked a turning point for the negative legacy surrounding me. I had invited some peers over for tea at our house when my father entered the hosting room where we were playing cards.

Life did not place barriers for me. These barriers were set by those closest to me. My father wanted me to be a replica of himself. He left angrily, returned with a pomegranate stick in hand, and began stinging my guests while berating me: "A thousand times I told you: this is a guesthouse, not a café!"

The first lessons he taught me were to imitate everything he did, from the snapping of his fingers and stroking of his mustache to his gait, posture, glances, face-washing, eye-rubbing, frowning, and pursing of lips in anger, contempt, or even admiration.

I spent the night anxious and worried. I thought about breaking free from this narrow confinement imposed on me—the village. Like any village, there was nothing but a tiny space to breathe. No cinema, no cafe, no sports club, nor any other kind of place for gathering socially. I only heard stories about the cafe, club, parks, and sea from others, sometimes the friends who visited the tailor shop's owner when I worked there. My main hobby was the cinema in Damascus, where I watched movies several times if I liked them.

Deciding I was no longer needed in the village, I asked my tailoring teacher if I could stay and sleep at the shop after work. He asked me the reason but I didn't tell the truth. Instead, I told him I was exhausted from riding my bike sixteen miles to and from the village every day.

On the inner wall opposite the shop's door, there was a small window that let in a bit of light and air. We only opened it during the summer.

At bedtime, I closed the shop's door and turned off the lights, but kept the window open. Everything within view through the window seemed clear. On a bedroom balcony in the neighboring building, a silk curtain in a sugar-like color ran down its window, striped with golden threads. I restrained myself from staring too long to discern further details.

I spread an English velvet cloth on the tailoring table under the window. That night, I stayed awake, troubled by my father's concerns and fears for me. He will surely regret what he did to me and my young guests; when I return, he will not repeat that act. Then, I slept until sunrise and the first rays of sunlight entered through the glass front.

The teacher asked me how I spent my night. I assured him I was safe and in complete comfort. With all the curiosity of someone who wants to discover a new world, I secretly peeked at the building's gate, which my window overlooked, hoping to see what every teenager dreams of seeing in a mysterious place where their imagined lover might be.

I didn't want her to be like the veiled girls from my village, only showing their faces, but rather like the girl I saw in an Egyptian movie on the big screen. With short hair and a skirt above her knees, she ran with her boyfriend on the beach. She disappeared behind a curtain and reappeared in a floral swimsuit.

—

In the morning, a tall man in a white dishdasha, a shemagh covering his head, and his black head-band's tassels hanging over his chest, stepped out of the building's door. He caught my attention because he was wearing shiny shoes. A woman in Gulf attire followed, along with a young girl wearing slightly lighter clothes than her mother. My teacher stared as the man opened the car door and said: "Oh, what a lucky man you are. Whoever has rice has spices. What a beautiful Cadillac."

That day, they did not return. The apartment, upon which my window looked, had its lights off. I assumed it was this family who lived there. I stayed up until after midnight, waiting for their return. Drowsiness took over after a long day of work. I dozed, but hope must always remain alive in such circumstances.

That family finally returned on Wednesday after-noon. A secret bird inside me spread its wings of joy and began flapping against the bars of the cage within my chest. Time passed, and night came. The room my anticipation overlooked lit up. I stay up late but discover nothing new.

Thursday night. Then Friday night. Our Friday is the day off, and I am alone in the shop. From outside the window, a crumpled page of an old Lebanese art magazine is thrown to me. I unfold it. It contains one Lira and words written in poor handwriting saying: "Please buy me an art magazine—any magazine—and throw it to the inner balcony!"

Swift as the wind, I went to the sidewalk bookstore near Victoria Bridge and bought two Lebanese magazines, Al-Maw'id and Al-Wa'd. That night I couldn't sleep. I took a risk and threw a note back to her after writing with trembling hands: "I love you." Then, the reckoning. Her father demanded me.

I approached shyly, while he slipped my note from his robe pocket. He asked, "Is this your handwriting, my son?" These few gentle words reassured me he meant no harm. He looked at me lovingly, asking my name, my father's name, where we lived, why I slept in the shop rather than going home, and what my father did for a living. An obscure apprehension hit me as I wondered: If his daughter fancied me, why would she not keep our exchange a secret? Or was there some discrepancy in her mind that led her to share it?

The matter did not end. My father sent one of our relatives to address the situation. I returned home and met my father, who seemed like a completely different person. He embraced me warmly for the first time, making me feel indescribable paternal warmth. He told me something contrary to the current reality: "My son, a pebble in its rightful place is worth a huge rock. Here too, there are girls; when they grow up, I will find you the most beautiful one to marry. This world has as many girls as there are stars."

Someone must have told him about my story with the neighbor of the shop and his daughter. Later, I found out that the Bey (Duke) was a friend of her father, and he must have been the one to inform my father about what the young girl's father wanted. I knew from his car's license plate that he was from the Gulf. However, I couldn't figure out the nature of his relationship with the Bey.

The world turned dark before my eyes. I became pessimistic—for a brief period—to the point where I saw some people, whom the Earth bore, as nothing but burdens, for they never considered restoring life to what it should be: healthy and righteous, unaffected by the wicked and tyrants. It was as if they were blind. If the thinkers who claim understanding were to read what the oppressed, persecuted, stifled, and deprived write on the walls of city restrooms and public parks, they would change many of their convictions. I am ashamed to document what was written. I try to draw some strength from our forefathers to write the blunt truth before they are wiped away by servants of these places.

Nothing is more painful for a villager than having their dream of a city disrupted; a city where they wish to see nothing but beauty, radiant faces, and high foreheads.

It wasn't long before I freed myself from the pessimism that had gripped me. Love creates wonders; this time, it saved me from embarking on a long, troublesome path.

Our neighbor was close friends with the wedding singer. They would go to work together, weeding and harvesting anise, and threshing its dried seeds. The tents where the anise threshing took place had a unique atmosphere. Our neighbor told me about the singer after she had escaped from a serious crime that her uncle had planned for her. She would talk and cry, her sobs subsiding as memories of their shared experiences came to the surface.

"She loved a young man – what's wrong with love? He promised her marriage, and in a moment of passion, she became pregnant. I don't call it a moment of weakness; rather, a moment of strength. A girl with the will to do what she wants is not weak. The problem was her lover. He was spineless, not facing the consequences of his actions like a real man should. He bowed to his father who refused to let him marry the woman he loved. To that father, love was a disgrace."

Fifty years after that personal tragedy struck the lovers, I met the singer's beloved, who had aged significantly. I reminded him of their love. He sighed, one that contained a volcano of emotions, hardly dormant. Nothing is more painful than a man's tears after regret and loss, the shattering of dreams, and the death of an irretrievable hope and irreplaceable love. The man wept, his copious tears unable to wash the dust accumulated during years away from those places where the sun once rose and set with his lover's face. People continued to sing her songs at weddings even after her departure. At the conclusion of his story, he said, "I was despicable."

Before goodbye, he choked on words I couldn't recognize. The same hand that once committed a despicable act of love wiped tears from his cheeks. It seemed to intensify the fire raging within.

Time passes, and stories rest within us, filled with unexpected twists never in our plans. Sometimes we reopen books of the past, even when we walk on a highway that was once a winding dirt road.

In your name, oh Love, many lovers walk your paths toward their demise. For some, love was but a curse. Many disbelieved you and were defeated. Many lost your guidance and strayed far away. Others only saw your carnal triangle and lost both body and soul—losing themselves in the process.

In the end, love is a power that intervenes between two people. It allows beauty to play its role and instinct to play its part, letting the deficiency in both conjure a genie that enchants one to the other—all driven by the desire for completion. This is where the game of love begins, a game no one has yet mastered. Love has been a small war waged on Earth and continues to be. Victors and vanquished alike are moved to tears by love.

A single smile might ignite this war, or a tear could extinguish it. Only those who have fled to the absolute, seeking salvation and enlightenment in nirvana or whatever is postponed by fate, have escaped it. As they fled, they paid a hefty price; they suffered torment, their sinews torn apart, and they were scorched. Yet they refused to repent or their repentance was not accepted. The enemies of love eternally judge them in every time and place.

It was nighttime. In the vast silence, only the sound of our footsteps, mine and my friend Hamza's, could be heard. He asked me, "Do you remember the person who caused the wedding singer's displacement, making her flee from the demons of this era?"

"Yes, I remember him. He is still crying," I said.

Hamza, as always, astonishes me and interprets the matter differently: "Those are, who failed to reach love. They claimed it was a disgrace or that the wind was against their ship's sails. So, they turned to promises of the hereafter and its women. They were left behind and went into oblivion. Are they winners or losers? Only God knows!"

"Your words remind me of the innocent blood that has been shed, as if unseen.

Could love be the cause, or is it something else?"

He firmly told me, "In a small village, if several murders occur (and he began counting on his fingers) involving the girls of so and so, and another, and another, and another... all within a period not exceeding two years; how many women are killed and their blood violated on this planet? Are all these crimes committed to cleansing the shame? Add to that the victims of wars, technology, hunger, and disease. Who will wash away all this disgrace from the Earth?"

Hamza is right. Perhaps I am also right in what I initially said according to my understanding. We returned to the story of the wedding singer. This time he agreed that historical context—influenced by thought, economy, means of production, religious beliefs, and spiritual experiences—guides the course of love, emotional relationships, instincts, and most importantly, the game of fate in sustaining life on Earth.

As for the crimes committed by masculinity against femininity, they are but a part of the story. Love, in the male perspective, is the stronger one overpowering the weaker through a secret snare. Over time, Eve became weaker after being crowned, for long durations, as a goddess or queen and worshipped under various names and guises.

Masculinity took advantage of her maternal periods, tamed her, domesticated her, and led her down a path from which she could not return. A path that leads her to a stagnant quagmire, an inevitable drowning if she continues to pursue what she desires. This is the game of fate in sustaining life on Earth.

CHAPTER TWELVE

**Don't lay the entire past in front of you;
it has many stumbling stones!**

I don't know what happens to me when I wake up. And how I surrender my head to puzzling daydreams filled with mysteries and secrets, and I see myself renewing the search for love and the herb of immortality. This spark will fade with time, for reasons one does not reveal while stubbornly fearing.

I scold myself to adapt, and such human adaptation means adjusting to the climates of life. It means being prepared to welcome the seasons and knowing in advance what you will do when facing heat or cold, for example. It is thus a product of the fear of nature's harm; similarly, adapting to phases of time where logic changes. Some people do not consider this, either out of ignorance or intentionally, causing an inevitable clash with oneself. What happens in the Third World also happens in any civilized world, or any world that claims to be civilized.

My friend Hani, who was called the Anise King by the workers in the anise fields due to his interest in cultivating this crop from seed to seed, emigrated to a foreign country to escape his sense of injustice. In his last message to me, he says, essentially:

"I escaped from the beast, I fell into a pit. Here too, I hold no value whatsoever, even though I am just like any other citizen. I respect the laws and aspire to a decent life. I feel like an unnecessary addition. I am treated as a stranger, an ignored person. They offer me jobs that they themselves wouldn't do. Work is not a disgrace.

"But you don't feel that they look at you through a religious lens unless you encounter a situation involving religion, and if that happens, all their fingers point towards you being Arab, Muslim, or involving more specific details such as Palestinian, Lebanese, Syrian, Yemeni or Iraqi. The details go even further: Sunni, Shia, Christian, Druze, and more: Levantine, from Beirut, Baghdad, or other regions in the Gulf. The list goes on and on with more distinctions.

"You cannot know what is in their minds until they embrace the wealthy of us, the educated, the young, or those who are hostile to their own country.

"The problem, my friend, is our feeling of lacking freedom, even though some of us are like medieval slaves whose freedom ends where their chain is bound around their neck! Each sinner here has their own chain. It may end at a house of worship, a brothel, a nightclub, a sidewalk to wander on, or a public park without shelter."

I continue reading the lengthy letter:

"I wonder to myself: Why did I decide to leave my country? I was forced into it.

"When you find someone who listens to you, they want something in return. I am a man and can manage my affairs through cunning or any method, even if it's dubious, always there are those who help justify; although our societies still entrust the justificatory mind with managing our world.

"Imagine if the person in need was a woman and she had nothing to offer? She is still considered subservient to men, marginalized, and without any role. She has not achieved economic freedom or taken her right to be her own master in managing her financial affairs or reproductive control. All the talk about her freedom granted by beliefs, ideologies, or human rights organizations is just ink on paper. She remains shackled in bondage, and that's all there is.

"Humanity has existed for tens of thousands of years, yet people in a world where their homeland is seen only in the sky don't care about belonging to land or citizenship among fellow humans who share their concerns in life and death."

—

Hamza arrived in the evening, as we agreed, to visit our friend Badr and congratulate him on being released from prison for political reasons.

My friend Hani's letter was still in my hands. Hamza asked me to let him read it. I handed it to him. His facial expressions changed according to what he saw: questions, admiration, or surprise. He finally lifted his head and said: "God works in mysterious ways! It would have been better for your friend not to migrate. Migration is not tourism. It's like uprooting a fruit-bearing tree to plant it elsewhere. Reply to him in your letter that 'a pebble in its rightful place is worth a rock,' as the saying goes."

On our way to visit Badr, we met Ramzi. He joined us and said, "Badr should have kept his tongue shorter. He lost two years of his life because of a trivial statement."

"You want him without principles," said Hamza.

"I think they made a fool of him and made him a scapegoat," Ramzi replied.

"You're only seeing the tail end of the story, Ramzi. There are bigger implications here, and I think you're unaware. They don't want anyone involved in a game that doesn't belong to them; or more accurately, they're not skilled as them."

"Badr became a prime example for others. Once his suffering in prison is revealed, it will serve as a lesson for you and others. What the small players don't know; politicians enjoy close ranks together while the small players fight among themselves like dogs over a bone. Their fighting subsides when the bone is taken away, and in the meantime, they await another round. Badr is small, very small in this game. He's like the size of a pinhead if not smaller."

Badr greeted us with a face—despite being cheerful upon our arrival—that seemed to convey regret, disappointment, or the loss of something.

His hospitality was dull. The only thing that slipped out about his two years in prison: "I was hung upside down for hours on end, from time to time."

Hamza said after we left, "You did well not to discuss anything sensitive in front of him. Prisoners like him are usually not released unless they commit to cooperating with their jailers."

Prison tales are like fingerprints; although numerous and repetitive, they can never be alike.

A decade later, fate chose Husni as my friend. In him, I found all the meanings of friendship: respect, loyalty, and love. Ironically, he was once a jailer.

I never found any two stories he told me alike, despite the similarities in the methods of extracting information from prisoners. Some of his tales left me speechless and kept me up at night. He would stay awake some nights until dawn, smoking, and brewing tea to drink, afraid that if he dozed off, nightmares would haunt him. He shared those nightmares. Poor friend Husni; I was heartbroken when we parted. Even now, I don't know anything about him.

How many prisons exist in this world that we know nothing about? The cruelest prisons are the cells, crueler are those cells that travel with us, and the cruelest of them all is the grand prison: our planet. There are many homes with inhabitants shackled by a reality where freedom is completely absent. The shackled person could be a woman, child, family head, servant, or even a slave. How many homes have no windows; no sunlight enters them nor air?

There was someone whose name I cannot mention, but many knew him. I didn't witness what happened. He was chained and tied to the main wood ceiling beam in a room, living in the most basic conditions. He was treated like a madman who couldn't be controlled, though some viewed him as sane. There must have been a reason for this man from my village to be in this state for two decades. The cause remained unknown, even when the man died. One morning, I heard the town crier hesitantly announce his death.

There was another man whose prison was open, but he had to sit from morning till evening on a rock planted in front of his family's gate. He was in his prime when he left the village during a famine to work in Lebanon. What he saw in Lebanon, called the "Switzerland of the East," in the early 1950s was something he never witnessed in our medieval-shaped and themed village.

When he returned from Beirut for the first time, I visited. He told me unbelievable things about women's freedom and men's respect for women. I couldn't comprehend it at that time. No doubt, he saw things with a biased perspective. Lebanon, like any country in our region, has more than diversity—it comprises various sects, open-minded people, and fundamentalists.

Before the unexpected storms of life scattered us, he was sitting on the same stone in front of his house when I last saw him. He had just returned from Beirut and lost everything he inherited from his father due to his siblings' greed.

The land, like many village properties at that time, had no formal ownership proof, only old unofficial agreements serving as sales contracts, property exchanges, or gifts from wealthy landlords to those displaced, relocated, or working as laborers.

He hadn't completely lost his mind yet, and his condition was still in its early stages. He recounted the places he worked in Lebanon until he settled in a job with an Armenian family in Beirut. Upon returning to the village, he lived with a Bye family. He told me what he knew about this family was unknown to anyone else. The man was well-regarded among influential politicians and the right-hand man of a high-ranking official. Nobody could determine his whereabouts: still in the country, Beirut, Damascus, Makkah, Haifa, Amman, or Jerusalem; but what I sensed is that their stay here was not permanent, and there may come a day when they'll be gone.

Eventually, that happened. The man left behind something that would foster a positive memory.

He donated properties to agents or farmers and built a school for the children. In all honesty, everything that his kind hands did for the village will ultimately come to nothing, and time will say, "Once there was a village here that vanished like a pinch of salt in an ocean!"

CHAPTER THIRTEEN

The wind does not return to the same place unless it is a whirlwind.

Nostalgia for the past, may compel you to remove the photo of the Mona Lisa from the wall and replace it with a picture of you, as a child playing in the mud.

September arrives, announcing the bounty of the seasons' crops. Tomorrow, the harvest will be gathered and stored in grain silos. The fields are completely empty, except for some leftover straw that will be used to insulate the goat pens during the winter. We rejoice as children, as we anticipate the Feast of the Cross. We find greater joy in it than in other celebrations where people exaggerate their rituals: Eid al-Adha and Easter. Unlike those feasts, there are no new clothes, sandals, sweets, or visits to relatives and neighbors during the Feast of the Cross. There is no need even to wish our parents a happy holiday, by kissing their hands, and there is no holiday bonus.

As the sun sets on the night of the Feast of the Cross, children gather in their respective neighborhoods in the open squares. The true essence of a child's freedom is manifested through play and preparation to ignite the sacred fire by collecting all types of firewood, from dry tree trunks to anise stalks, thorns, and fence shrubs. They search everywhere, for damaged bicycle tires or any rubber items like plastic, or rubber shoe heels, since these items stay alight for longer periods. The night of the Cross culminates with a visit to the northern sloped hill, where we pile everything flammable. We believed, this flame to be visible not only to us but also to the entire world from the highest peaks we have chosen, symbolizing the light of the Cross.

This childhood act inspired the youth to ignite their passions, motivating them to reach greater heights and they firmly refused to take us with them to their celebrations.

As children, we used to repeat these rituals without knowing their meanings. All we wanted was for the fire to sweep away the darkness of the night with its light. The bigger and stronger the blazing fire, the further we could see. We were happy when the wind blew upon it, making it more intense and fiercer. We competed by jumping over the fire from one side to another.

Our enthusiasm increased when older youth joined us and invaded our atmosphere.

What united us with this Feast of the Cross with jumping-over-fire rituals despite our diverse faith composition as a social class, that believes in intellect, incarnation, wisdom, Greek philosophy, and everything related to monotheism since creation's beginning until today?

As children grow, so do their questions. I recall many memories, both sweet and bitter. What pains me most is that my convictions have remained unchanged because nothing has challenged or transformed them—particularly, the suffering this country has experienced due to division, hatred, and resentment. Had we all been aware of the reason behind it, we would have been as united as honey and crème. There have always been hidden hands playing games with us.

In the secrets of childhood: "After the Feast of the Cross, as he visited us yearly, Maundy Thursday paid his visit, a celebration indeed for childhood. Bringing from Damascus to the village square during the festival, were sellers of paper airplanes, cotton candy, colorful beads, toy whistles, and primitive fireworks—usually procured through barter. We traded hard-boiled eggs that had been cracked in a playful competition on

Maundy Thursday, in exchange for the seller's goods. Um Taysir, was the only woman selling homemade sweets during the holiday along with some other items that her husband, a night watchman, had brought from town in preparation for the feast day."

Driven by our love of life and attachment to the past's beauty, we carry our childhood with us to our final resting place like a talisman that rescues us from disappointments and missteps. How often do we resort to it to delay despair or chase away nightmares of aging prematurely? Just as I am doing now.

It could rightly be called the Feast of Anise, as without the season of this plant and the income it generates, there would be no money to buy holiday clothes and sweets. Without it, this day would be like any other day.

After that season, a young girl broke like a tender willow. Her grandmother would call me and my cousin, Ayoub, secretly from among the other children to give us some honey, dripping with sweetness. I saw that girl with her grandmother, watching us as she helped with the beehives made from clay by her grandmother. I once saw her cry when she was stung by a bee. Her crying was nothing compared to the tears she shed when she was married off as a bride at the age of ten.

We played as kids at her wedding with tambourines, among the women who danced. We had fun tying their shawls, which dangled down to their waists and receded from their heads, laughing when they discovered it. The young bride wept, her situation similar to many others in a village that seemed destined to lose its identity. The bride went to her groom's house, and there, it didn't take long for the sun of her childhood to set. She was a little mare facing a big horse. Even after twenty years, tongues still wag with tales of her life, death, and those who followed in the same footsteps.

Tales are adorned, and when they become uglier or more beautiful, they acquire the permanence of existence in time, or they do not exist at all. Or they remain as a gamble. And, of course, it happens that spices are sprinkled on some.

Weddings have their secrets. Some are easy to disclose and reveal, while others remain timeless and never expire, granting you the right to mention them.

Whatever is destined for someone else cannot be yours, and vice versa. Fate is the strongest player in the game of our existence. We are but small operatives in its hands. So, say the commandments, mirrors, tablets, and stars; and we must not follow our desires or believe our dreams, nor what philosophy and technology tell us. We must be like the mill's mules in the game of fate.

Tales are many as numerous as the grains of sand in the deserts.

CHAPTER FOURTEEN

Your feet don't care
About the traces they leave
On the paths they tread!

Between love and affection, there is a thin thread connecting them; however, it quickly breaks when affection does not acknowledge the actions of lovers following their instincts. Likewise, lovers view affection as a space for their wings to soar in worlds of fantasy, with romanticism that allows them to experience love and immerse themselves in physical manifestations to the point of madness. Then, nature takes its turn, imposing its beauty in every aspect of its language.

It's no wonder that a village goes to the city to sell its anise, mint, wheat, goat milk, cream, and tomatoes, instead of the city coming to it. The city determines product prices, taxes, and chooses what the village cultivates— even poppy and hemp (used until the mid-20th century to sedate crying infants).

My uncle and others planted poppy hidden among anise plants in the spring. This strategy prevented gossipers from taking notice and loose tongues from spreading such secrets. Poppy was prohibited; however, a segment of society demanded it, just like the poor asked for falafel. Moreover, hemp was cultivated in other villages around the Damascus countryside to meet the demand for rope-making, crop nets, and animal feed bags. It was legally licensed for these purposes but also was trafficked for narcotic manufacturing or used secretly by addicts.

Muhannad, who worked at a nightclub, told me about addicted customers. He was once afflicted like them but recovered. A girl from the village he loved had demanded he quit. He succeeded twice in overcoming addiction and found love. However, he became addicted to the boiled anise drink, which is not a sin. As we grew older and frequented the city for work and exploration, I realized that Muhannad's job at the nightclub was more about compensating for his repression toward women and their pleasures than any other job he tried. In it, you see everything distilled, aged, and fermented—all related to women.

Damascus was not only the dream of our childhood, but also the dream of our ancestors and invading enemies.

With the brains of butterflies, we went to the city, our ethereal city since our great-grandparents migrated to it, and then settled in its southern part. But cities are like rivers; they never stay the same. Winters come and bring with them all that the seasons have accumulated in dust. They become polluted, or are invaded by floods or deluges. Much of what is prevalent or settled in them changes. And what has changed remains a sign for forthcoming times.

We do not know the blood that mixed with ours since our roots extended into it—perhaps we were forced to do so. The god Hadad received early newcomers to Sham (Damascus) in ancient times, opening his heart. He granted blessings, and the land was theirs. What time says about Damascus, and what it has suffered throughout the ages, has made it an eternal sanctity for us, even if our childhood did not wander through its alleys, neighborhoods, streets, and squares. We did not pick any Naranj, bitter oranges, from its gardens. We did not play with water from its lakes. We did not smell its Damask Roses nor its jasmine climbing on its walls.

Our childhood innocently entered Damascus, connected by thin but strong threads that stretch like gold and never break. I am one of those who entered this city, where my love for a girl of the rose district transformed into a phobia that took root in my head and never left, neither during day nor night. The ultimate conclusion I reached is that love without union is madness. The loved woman in our imagination differs immensely from reality.

After that, my imagination painted a picture of a singer, as if she were a mermaid. The only way for me to reach her was to write her a song, and to obtain her address through a journalist obsessed with writing about celebrity news. The task cost me nothing but the price of a cup of coffee at the Brazil Cafe in Damascus. I was unsuccessful in this endeavor too. I rang the bell of the building. A gate, like the entrance to a bohemian cave, opened, and a dog barked from behind the door. My singer appeared in the middle of her work, but I saw nothing else. All I knew was that the music violently shook the building, its walls, balconies, and roads. Above me, below me, and all around me, my strength and nerves faltered. I shattered like broken glass in the middle of the street. The game ended with repentance until the last moments of life, renouncing the hoped-for love and what our whims could do to us in a moment of recklessness and pride.

Nevertheless, as a villager, one must expect mistakes at every moment or else they will not escape dire consequences. After being afflicted with the desire to write, I visited a newspaper that publishes a story every week. I personally handed the editor-in-chief a short story and later mailed him three more stories. I waited a long time, but no stories were published. So, I decided to visit the editor-in-chief to inquire.

I would like to say: "I handed you my story; 'Your House is Burning, Juha,' more than a year ago and mailed you three more short stories: 'The World is Moving Backward,' 'Anise Girls,' and 'I am the Princess of This Country.' What has become of these stories?"

When I arrived, his office was crowded with visitors. I sat down after saying hello. Fortunately, the visitors left. A picture of his little daughter looked at me from under the glass cover of his desk.

His eyes watched my facial expressions. My forehead dripped with sweat. Unable to find a paper tissue in my pocket, he quickly pulled one out from a box on his right. As he busied himself arranging papers and files, I waited for him to speak. He didn't.

So, I asked, "What is the fate of my stories, sir? No one knows anything about them except you, your subconscious mind, your desk drawer or cabinet, or perhaps your wastebasket!"

His phone rang. He picked up the receiver, as if escaping a trap.

"Hello. Hi, my friend... No. No. No, I don't forget anything. Everything is programmed in my memory. Yes. I'm waiting for your article in the next issue. Always write to us.

We think that if everyone looked at the world from our own perspective, we could put an end to all the mistakes occurring on this planet."

I glanced out the window. The September sun was a pale yellow.

He'd hung up but the phone rang again right away.

"Hello, my friend. London is determined to leave the European Union. Yes. The third world swallows this knife. No, you're exaggerating a bit. Hello! Raise your voice a little; it seems like the line got disconnected."

The office boy entered. The editor stood as if saluting the flag.

"I didn't ask for you!" the editor said.

The office boy looked at me dejectedly and left.

Again, the phone rang. He answered: "I've been waiting for your work for some time now, my friend."

I understood that a woman was talking to him, although he pretended to be speaking to a man. I deliberately ignored it. I lifted a daily newspaper in my hand, unfolded it, and pretended to read.

"That man is not that scary," he said.

He meant her husband.

"The chalets solve the problem only in summer! Will you write the column tomorrow?"

His fingers froze on the headset. His face turned pale. He gently placed the headset down, then unconsciously shuffled some papers. He got up and walked around the table, taking a sip of water from a nearby glass. He tried to loosen his tie. I felt him suffocating.

The phone rang again. He looked at it angrily, not caring about the ringing.

"The telephone is the problem of all problems. One must devote time to answer it, my brother. What would happen if such an annoying device was never invented?"

The phone stopped ringing momentarily but then started again. He reluctantly picked up the headset, looking somewhat irritated.

"Hello. Welcome. You are the best accountant. You don't have to worry about the details of the sales committee. I am busy now; call at another time."

He put the handset down irritated. "Ugh!"

I raised my finger like a student.

"May I speak with you for a moment, professor? I have some short stories."

He interrupted.

"Your stories are important to us. However, providing them always comes at an inconvenient time. Our editors have more pressing concerns on their minds. Moreover, advertisements take priority. Newspapers rely on ads and cannot function without them. The only content that truly imposes itself is the crossword section. Dozens of phone calls come in when this corner is absent. Its editor is the most pampered one. He's the only person we cannot afford to mess with.

"We are now on the cusp of the winter season. This means we will miss half of our crossword followers!

You are an old friend. Your fingerprints in literature and journalism are unmistakable, and you know that the 'Horoscope' section has taken the top spot in newspapers and magazines.

"It's not just for entertainment; a smart editor can bring comfort and reassurance to readers. The problem is that we already have the required editor."

So how can I help you? Think with me for a moment. I understand each of our needs for additional income.

I found it. I found it. Expanding horoscopes is an important issue. What if you made the reader wait for a lost or misplaced hope? Love that was hidden or disappointed? Think about it carefully. Cover a different zodiac column each week—once for men, once for women, once about wealth, once about love, once about status, and once about the future.

"If you agree with that. We are now in September. Start with the birthdays of this month."

He noticed me looking at the page with disdain. He continued mockingly.

"Hah, I remembered. You have stories to the extent that worms, sorry, moth larvae will eat. Excuse me here is the story 'A Horse Whose Rider I Am' Oh no, 'A Princess of Land I Belong To.' No No, 'Anise Girls.'" He opened the drawer and took out various papers.

"Here's the story. Put another title on it. Instead of 'Anise Girls,' make its title 'Anise Plants.' And feel free to do so!"

CHAPTER FIFTEEN

However the night gets dark,
It cannot prevent a star
From shining.

Disappointment makes you return to the station from which you started, enabling your wings to carry you to fly again.

I thought that all minds worked without selfishness or greed, yet one day the tailor who taught me fired me without reason and replaced me with someone for a lower wage. That's the whole story. It was evening on that day when he waved goodbye, and I no longer held any value in his eyes. All wounds caused by money—according to him—must heal simply and without leaving scars. So, it was the money.

I found myself, at 14 years old, alone in the city center, circling like a mill mule: the wind howling and thunder roaring, snatching away the noise and hustle from the streets. I stood in front of Dunia

Cinema with warmth and the scent of people emanating from it. Those pouring into the cinema were there either because they were intrigued by the film or to pass time. It doesn't matter I already watched the movie: a cowboy gang terrorized the town with their crimes; however, the heroic sheriff prevailed—as in all movies—and defeated its members with his infallible guns that never run out of bullets, and the town lived in safety!

If I had to choose that night, between watching a movie or getting a crumb of bread, I would have chosen the bread crumb. My stomach was growling in hunger and cold. The most important thing in the world for me was to find a place to take refuge and spend the night. My pockets were empty, but they sheltered my hands from the biting cold that gnawed. My chest shivered, as fear of the unknown and the cold mixed with my nerves.

I imagined that all the currents of air passing through the city gathered to pass through my pant legs. My right pocket had a hole, and I would run my fingers through it to measure the temperature of my body. The pores of my skin were open, allowing the passing air to flow like an arrow toward my heart. My employer had locked the door before I could grab my leather jacket, which I usually take off when I start work, and in it was what remained of my wages.

I was still in the city center, the storm intensifying. Hailstones fell, bouncing and stinging like shards of glass. My employer appeared in my mind, as did the place where I used to work. It now seemed to me cold like a spider's den, once a warm haven where my childhood would toil from sunrise to midnight, where I would spread my blanket, which my employer doused in kerosene when I protested my wage reduction and then burnt in the street.

I lay what's left of that blanket in the middle of the cutting table and slept to the sound of a large wooden Pye-brand radio. Next to me was a small wooden crate where I saved some canned food and whatever was left over from my meals. The street turned into dirty little ponds. The air slapped me and a passing car splashed me, cleaning my face of what clung to it. The cold seeped into my bones. Hunger left my stomach hollow. The big voracious square mouths on the streets were sealed tightly, guarding someone's treasures—sweaters, coats, furs, heaters, pastries, sweets, grinders, drills, saws, and nails.

Soft hands opened them every morning to devour greedily, transforming everything into bundles of cash and checks.

Brrr. I curled my hands. I blew on them; other times I wiped what my body exuded through my nose. Panting. Running. Steps. Arms. Brains. Moans. Pleas. Tears. Burning nerves—all connected by invisible chains to that square mouth of iron, where the lifeline extends from and to.

I had one goal: to find a place where I could take refuge. I was not in a village where I could knock on any door. Here, the doors were like those of castles, and the windows too. The windows had four barriers: the stained glass, the curtains, the iron bars, and the lampshades. You wouldn't see even a glimpse of light coming from them, nor a single ray escaping to the street. No human scent could be detected. I would have loved to knock on any door, but I knew that would be like head-butting a rock; they were secured so well that one could not hear either a scream or a cry for help.

It was none other than my childhood friend, Muhannad, from my village, who was drawn to the city, working in one of its nightclubs. He would return every Friday, dressed in a tie and suit, to spend time with his family in the village.

He was the first to clash with the village's Sheikh. The Sheikh, upon smelling something other than

aniseed—the scent of wine mixed with other odors—
told him, "Give up alcohol; it is the filth of Satan." I
feared the Sheikh's anger if he knew I spent my night
at Muhannad's nightclub. I quietly thought: I am still
fourteen years old. No one will hold me accountable.
I will enter the club, lay my head on some table, and
sleep. But then I realized that sleep doesn't come easily
to those who are hungry, cold, or scared. No matter—I
will sleep. Along with hunger, cold, and fear come
angels who replace nightmares with beautiful dreams.

I passed another cinema door. A Texas cowboy
made of paper was on display. His feet dangled in the
air, his gun aimed at the street. His hat rose to the first
floor. He remained as I saw him during the day. The
rain didn't affect him; he was tightly fastened to the
wall, protected from above by a wide concrete ledge. I
briefly stopped at his legs, noticing that his boots lined
up with my face and his whip was above my neck before
continuing my walk toward an unknown destination.

It was almost midnight. Who would believe that a
child frequents a nightclub? Surely, I would be expelled
by the doorman.

"What do you want, boy?" he asked. "Ah! You're
the one who stole the bottles of Arak yesterday!"

I calmly controlled my nerves. "Now is not the time for jokes. Take me to Mohannad, who works here!"

"Mohannad? He's inside."

Mohannad stood with a heavily makeup-clad woman in a dimly lit area. I bet her mother wouldn't recognize her. So, this is the romantic atmosphere I've heard so much about. A man in a white jalabiya passed, emitting a scent similar to anise. No doubt, this is the 'Arak' I've also heard about.

Warmth flowed through my clothes and into my bones. Mohannad was surprised to see me. We shook hands.

"Your hands are cold. Do you want something?" he asked with great tenderness.

I smelled the scent of herbs, alfalfa, wild chamomile, mint, and jujube. Sweet childhood memories came to mind.

"I just need a place to spend the night. I have nowhere else to go."

The music volume increased slightly. Tension built. The club seemed to spin around me. Customers collided with each other in the crowd like barrels, their eyes hungrily following the women.

I didn't expect what Muhannad said: "However, this is a nightclub, not a... There's dancing, artists, drunkards, and..."

The fig leaf fell. The screws of my head were loosening. Two men in white jalabiyas sat at a nearby table. One of them stared at me. The other clapped. Muhannad ran toward him like a rabbit. He bowed. Another waiter clapped. Another waiter bowed. A third waiter bent. The bows continued.

Muhannad passed, carrying a tray of Arak bottles. He opened it, revealing the pungent smell that filled the room. The fragrance of aniseed wafted through my mind, and girls carried their green clusters to the roofs to dry under the sun.

Muhannad forgot or ignored his fellow villager. With the weather outside, I worried my clothes wouldn't allow me to spend a night on the streets. The warmth stopped circulating in my body.

Once again, the car wheels erased the traces of my footsteps. I leaped like a frog. Muhannad's face escaped me. The buildings surrounded me. I stopped at a corner. I heard someone yelling from the darkness.

"Thief! Stay where you are, or I'll shoot!" he said.

A night guard emerged from the darkness. My chest trembled, blending with a new guest—fear. My legs could no longer carry my small body. The guard ran toward me. He shook me and I vanished between his sturdy hands.

"I'm just passing through, I swear."

I told him the story of losing my job. He believed me. He was kind. He couldn't find a way to help me, except to direct me to another night guard from our village.

"Abu Diab is my friend," he said. "Go to him, he is a reliable man."

He was responsible for guarding one of the main axes of the city center. He was a reliable person. I remember his small yet vital orchard, the anise fields he cared for, and the beautiful anise-threshing tent.

His barren, dry field was now like the rest of the dry fields, its owners lured by the glass facades in the city. Flimsy dresses. Men who think like butterflies, are attracted by the mirage-like lights.

Abu Diab took off his coat and wrapped me in it. He ignited the firewood he had stored, although it was damp, and the fire hardly caught. He asked: "Why did you leave your family?"

The telephone wires whistled, the wind howled through my veins, and the rain poured like streams.

The wind extinguished the fire. I shivered again. Abu Diab blew on the embers, which glowed. The fire came back to life.

I ask him, "And why did you leave?"

A drunken man crossed the street and stopped, reeking of alcohol mixed with aniseed. He stared at us for a long time before asking the guard:

"Is this the right way, man?"

Shortly after, a patrol checked on us and questioned the guard about my presence with him.

"He's my son!"

He cursed and swore, standing firm. With determination, he told them that I would stay even if the sky falls on the earth.

He approached the trash barrel, emptied it, cleaned it, and rolled it toward me. He removed the waterproof waxed coat and spread it on the inner wall of the barrel while positioning its opening close to the fireplace. Wrapping my feet in his woolen scarf, he blew on the fire. The flames reflected a warm glow. He told me tales of the city's night—about rascals, thieves, and drunks. Sleep left my eyes. The firewood ran out.

He stirred the ashes with his finger, causing embers to flare. Searching through his pockets, he found a few papers. He looked at them closely and took out a white cloth handkerchief. He threw the papers and handkerchief into the embers. A thin smoke rose, followed by a brief flare-up.

Pulling a small cardboard slip from his inner pocket, he looked at me with a smile:

"Not this one, No!"

I began shivering again. He lifted me out of the barrel. The barrel's iron was still warm. I wished to roll the barrel through the streets to wake up the city. The guard looked at the horizon with an assured demeanor.

"It's the night's end; soon dawn will rise," he said.

CHAPTER SIXTEEN

Resurrection, and the end of the world!

As the fate of anise and its journey comes to an end, some of it becomes part of the liquor family, undoubtedly contributing to a person's path toward an unfavorable end. Perhaps to hell, as believed by religious extremists. Based on this belief, any extremist could condemn this vice. There is always fear of the hereafter that lurks within everyone.

How our innocence has let us down, and the minds of butterflies residing in our heads, young and old. So many sayings related to the afterlife dominate what we should believe in and dictate earthly rituals. These sayings affect our existential journey. "Work for your worldly life as if you'll live forever, and work for your afterlife as if you'll die tomorrow."

There is always someone watching, monitoring even the breaths that leave our chests, for purposes that are likely counter to our future, prophecies might be a rich fodder for them. Many of these end-of-the-world prophecies have been disproven by science, despite attempts to either confirm or debunk them using scientific means. Poets, astronomers, and fortunetellers come next after those extremists, only to be let down by the unseen world as well.

The prophecies that come from religious leaders are easily believed because of the ignorance residing in the minds of one-dimensional people. They believe that whatever the religion or its representatives say is the truth. They disregard other truths, even if they have passed through laboratories, or have been observed through the lenses of physics, chemistry, atomic science, or even humanities like philosophy, history, economics, politics, and more.

I didn't often pay much attention to who visited our house. Yet a Lebanese clergyman visited us one spring during the 1950s. I knew he was Lebanese based on his accent, which was different from the familiar Syrian intonations.

It was a sunny day in May, and my father, my aunt's husband, and my uncle were sitting on small chairs against a wall in the dirt courtyard. The man asked to sit where they were sitting, and said there was no need to host him in a room. I hovered around them just to listen to his accent, which fascinated me with its musicality. Unlike our village accent, his speech had those sweet undulations that appealed to me.

The man started talking, and I listened intently.

"I come on behalf of the leader of our sect in Lebanon," he said.

He took out a message from his robe and handed it to my aunt's husband.

"Please read it," he said.

They looked at him sheepishly and glanced at each other with disappointment. My aunt's husband returned it to him, saying, "Would you please read it to us?"

"I don't want to impose on you," the clergyman said. "One of you can read it."

"It's our bad luck, Sheikh. None of us can read," my uncle said. "Maybe my brother can figure out some letters. Just read it, please."

The visiting Sheikh unfolded the letter. It was written in calligraphy, like other handwritten religious manuscripts. He cleared his throat and began speaking without looking at the message.

"The letter says that the Day of Judgment will come, God willing, on August 6 of this year."

He folded the letter and put it back in the envelope, before handing it to my aunt's husband.

"You must inform our brothers that Judgment Day is coming," he continued, "and everyone must hold firm to their faith. They should prepare for the Day of Judgment with pure hearts and clear consciences for this great day!"

He glanced toward the room where my father stored the anise until he could sell it to a merchant.

"I smell something objectionable. The scent of anise liquor?" he said.

"Yes. It is just anise," my father said. "This is our main crop that sustains us, Sheikh!"

"It is not permissible for the day of the end to come, that this is in someone's house! It heralds ruin, hellfire, and a terrible fate."

My father was unsure how to respond, so he simply said, "May God help us!"

I spread the news of Judgment Day among my peers, and they, in turn, passed it on, spreading it through the village before it was officially announced by that Sheikh.

A Christian holiday was approaching, but they believed the resurrection story from a non-Christian cleric because trust between us is mutual in anything that a religious man says. After the news broke, people refrained from preparing for the holiday, waiting for August 6.

To my knowledge, my uncle was the only one who did not believe in those predictions. A day before we heard the clergyman's warning of Judgment Day, I heard him telling his father—who represented agricultural affairs for Bey—in a hushed voice without my understanding the meaning or context.

"Bey was in Jerusalem and didn't come here immediately," he said. "He traveled from Jerusalem to Mecca and did not pass through Damascus this time."

CHAPTER SEVENTEEN

Conditional love

does not help a person

to be proactive

Nothing in existence can balance the scale of dis-appointments and losses except love, which was waiting for me to dispel all the sorrow, loss, and frustration weighing upon me. It was love's pulse that drew me closer whenever I tried to escape it. Undoubtedly, a teenager must be prepared for anxiety, sleeplessness, productive and unproductive thinking, moving forward with determination toward the trap of entanglement. It is that primitive trap set by love for teenagers, and maybe adults as well.

To fall in love means to surrender your neck to the one who will either adorn it with flowers or thorns. You must bear your cross and ascend to the Golgotha of love without looking back, for only then will it possess the quality of permanence.

Falling into that trap means you'll grant your soul to fly in a space you didn't choose. That's what my wings have been telling me since the first day they fluttered involuntarily toward a human form different from mine in its terrain. It's the secret that radiated like a light escaping from a dazzling sun. You must forget who you are, or close your eyes and shield your heart from what you see; but you cannot. You should have been born with no eyes, with no ears, with no nerves, and without any senses to achieve an undesired salvation.

The scent of green anise drifted from her clothes when I embraced her for the first time. I later understood why anise crops were taken to distant lands, as if we cultivated what was permissible only for it to later become forbidden. I knew how a lover could spin around and go dizzy with the rotation of the Earth without falling.

The fragrance of anise was not everything. My girlfriend carried the smell of the earth more when she lay on the dry ground that hadn't tasted water. The anise, too, was deprived of it during the final stages of ripening.

How much my mother loved Suha, perhaps secretly wishing she would become her daughter-in-law. My mother would sigh sometimes. I later learned Suha was promised to one of her relatives, who proposed to her. One can defy anything in our village, except love; those who had dared to pay the price with blood. Suha slipped out of my wings, and all that remained was the euphoria left by anise, coursing through every cell of my body. A euphoria with the power of a flame, burning many pages written by the days in the record of life.

It is difficult for a teenager to break from adolescence in a closed environment like a medieval village, unless they are forced into marriage and confined within a narrow circle. This circle consists of their closed household with family members, including their father, mother, siblings, siblings' spouses, and children, as well as an open field, goat or sheep pen, and stable for animals. Amidst this siege, the teenager seeks solace by exploring their curiosity about the opposite sex and searching for loopholes to flee from the thorny societal constraints.

Girls were not luckier, but much worse because the knife is on the road waiting. Suha's mind was not with her husband, and the mind that follows emotion here walks in a minefield, or a thorny one, in normal circumstances. I once received a message from Suha through an old woman who had a long history in paving roads for lovers to meet safely. I later learned that the fee she received from Suha to deliver the message was expensive—a towel, a skirt cover, and floral pants. Suha's message was on a piece of paper cut from her third-grade elementary school notebook.

She said in disconnected words, like chicken scribbles: "I do not forget the days when we used to meet between anise fields. I wished I could be your wife. I do not forget how you squeezed me and felt like fainting. You didn't notice when I gasped and melted in your hands."

The message looked as if written with trembling hands—hands that still have the scent of anise in fields devastated by drought, while there are those hands who've paved the way for a future without anise.

I talk about anise because it is the only crop in the village that people rely on for money. It enables them to visit the city, buy clothes, and shoes for the holidays, farming equipment, and groceries like sugar, coffee, and rice. Farmers and merchants—store agricultural crops—just like cats and mice. Some evenings, farmers engage in discussions about what to plant this year.

Anise is an annual crop, but often when the purchasing season ends, merchants raise the prices for a limited number of farmers. This serves as an incentive for others to cultivate larger areas in the coming seasons. Consequently, there is an abundance of produce that subsequently leads to a decrease in price compared to the previous year.

I witnessed such situations throughout my childhood but couldn't comprehend them until I grew up and became one of those affected by these games.

It was my mistake, due to my naivety one season, that I convinced my father to follow the merchant's advice to increase the cultivation area of okra, beans, and some other vegetables at the expense of anise. As a result, only three farmers planted large areas of anise and obtained the highest price that year. To clarify further, the price per pound was five lira before that year and increased to eight lira the following year. Worse still, the entire village planted relatively large areas of okra and eggplants, causing their prices to plummet. Once I picked a small carload of eggplant and went to the vegetable market; I stayed there until the end of the day, unable to find a buyer. I reduced the price per kilogram to ten piasters and then shouted: "Who will unload this cargo and take it for free?"

One merchant said: "I'll take it on the condition that you give it to me with its bags and help me unload it!"

Despite those painful lessons, my father did not agree to open a shop for me in the city after I learned sewing. My intuition told me he wanted me close by, so I could continue to help him with the farming during my free time and the required seasons.

One winter day, I returned from work to find the anise merchant standing across from my father, negotiating intensely.

"I deserve your anise more than anyone else. I am a son of this village!" the merchant insisted.

"But you didn't pay the price others did," my father replied.

"But the imported merchant didn't pay more than that!"

"That's not my fault!"

"The importer knows the village farmers are generous with me. They give me their anise at a reasonable price since I lend to them without interest for a whole year until harvest season!"

"I didn't borrow from you; I borrowed from strangers at interest so I wouldn't have to owe you or anyone else."

I was tired, so I left them. The following year, on my day off, I saw that merchant carrying a steelyard on his shoulder and calling out to my father.

"I came!" he said.

I learned the details a year later. That merchant had lent money to my father when our anise harvest was poor and barely covered the amount we had borrowed.

My father was like a shuttle, going in and out of the house. I couldn't stand in his way to ask what was bothering him. He was sad, tense, and angry. I figured he was battling the entire universe that day. In the evening, he said, "Come with me."

I followed him into the sitting room. He stared at me intently, placed his hand on my shoulder, and spoke softly, "All our lives here have been full of misery. Focus on your profession, your work, and get back to your studies, my son. Here we remain as we are. We work like mules of burden, eating the leftovers from the season. We eat its waste; everyone takes a bite out of us. Even the goats or the airspace we breathe in—we pay for it all, taxes and all. It's like a nightmare haunting us in our sleep." He fell silent for a while before resuming with a heavy sigh and a bitter question: "What's your weekly salary?"

I didn't hesitate to answer, as he had never before asked about my work salary: 280 piasters. "I need you to spare me 250 piasters. Don't be upset; I'll make it up to you when you're wedded. Your mother needs a doctor and medicine. Her illness is severe. The Bey suggested a skilled doctor named Marcel."

My hand ran into my pants pocket, and I took out my entire earnings. I kissed him on the forehead and placed the money in his jacket pocket. For the first time, I saw a gleam in his eye—followed by tears that flowed abundantly as he wiped them with his palm while praying for my life to be as I wished, turning dust to gold in my grasp. After calming himself, he said, "I wish I could meet your factory owner where you work. Anyway, tell him, 'My father sends his regards!'"

My father left, and I remained in the room after he asked me not to go out. I heard the rumbling of the gas stove coming from the pantry that we used as a kitchen. After a while, my father returned carrying a teapot and two cups, with steam seeping from under the teapot's lid as if it were trying to explode. My father's smile that day was yellow, and withered enough to create an autumn where all the leaves in our village would fall.

CHAPTER EIGHTEEN

The most beautiful flowers are

those that grow amidst

the ashes.

I had to return home before sunset. I took the path that led to our house. Memories crowded my mind, stretching back to my early years, receding into the depths of time of the village.

My memory stopped at a period when I thought Mount Qasioun was the edge of the world, as it clashed with clouds, lightning, and muddy streams passing by doorsteps. Back then, nothing shook my world except the roar of thunder and my father's fury. Paths wound around fields, turned over by a Babylonian-style plow. I embarked on a long journey that led me to the heart of the city with my eyes closed, only believing in things when I touched them with my fingers.

That path brought me to a sewing machine, which I still carry—and it carries me. I bear its consequences, as it bears mine. Its threads still tighten my nerves like bowstrings on a primitive warrior's wooden bow. Its shuttle takes me to Sisyphus' rock or one overlooking an ever-ready sea waiting to greet those willing to become food for its tiny colorful fish. Ready to play Orpheus' lyre in fields that once bloomed with anise flowers, daughters dancing to its melancholy tunes. The hum of the sewing machine takes me far away from people, those who pile up like matchsticks in a box with set dimensions and others who float like corks in shallow waters.

The train of time carries me until I stop at its first station. I pick up my disappointment from the tracks that were cut off a long time ago. I stand lost, bewildered, astray, and despondent. Soft sand is beneath my feet moving. Before my eyes are a mirage, a nebula, storms, and tremors, the hardest was the aftershocks.

A new day's work begins. I return to my sewing machine and grumble at it, taking out my frustration on its weathered gray metal.

The Earth awakens periodically to the footsteps of barbarism, crushing everything in its path. It sows thorns among the homes of brothers and their fields, planting hostility, grudges, division, hatred, animosity, schemes, sect-related disputes, and religious differences. It is cruel to see everything before you in a color of scorn, and everyone around you opposing the open air.

—

At the beginning of that day, I felt as if I was at war. With no truce or cease-fire, and no end to this battle. The space tightened around me, as did the world. I left the shop, before getting down, and found myself on that same street, where I amused myself by calculating distances between cars, reading their plate numbers by observing what was written on their rear bumpers and windows. There were phrases glorifying everything sacred or addressing a beautiful lover, lost sweetheart, hopeful lover, the bashful neighbor's daughter, or a pretty singer.

I cracked my knuckles, hoping to dispel the heavy air that weighed down the wings of my spirit. These tired wings carried the burdensome, indispensable damages in a time when everything becomes poorer. I was tired of bearing postponed ambitions and hopes that resided in the head, heart, and eyes. Hopes that seeped into my feet, were sticky and viscous. Then, just before reaching teenage completion, they turned into a mass of lead.

The hum of my sewing machine shares my sorrow. It accompanies me in my solitude, or through long nights where the stars reveal their nightmares to me.

How many things have changed in the times with my machine, as I revolved like a mill mule around the same axis, in an era that flows at the speed of light, far away from me, with its philosophies, its sciences, its roaring machines, its satellites, its space stations, its computers, its domination, and its visible and invisible powers? An era in which all I have witnessed closely are its bullets, murders, and bloodshed, an unfair justice weighed by the shackles of slaves and tainted with hostility, resentment, and oppression.

I reached my sewing machine one distant day in my scattered childhood, with a fragrance that dissipates in God's space, transforming into a grief-repelling drink and false hopes that deceive oneself by thinking everything is fine and makes the head more likely to be a closed reservoir for all concerns and wrong decisions intended to be postponed forever, in a city that was completed by gathering opposites that meet only over power, money, and women.

The day I reached my sewing machine, I didn't know it would try to steal the scent of green meadows and tall trees, try to cleanse me of my village's intoxicating odor as well as the fragrance of its girls and aniseed, which never fades. What I do know is that I carried my sewing machine in a sluggish era. Its void is profound, its mazes suffocating, and its paths blocked. I carried it with me in that era, along with its sad, harsh buzzing, and my wounded cry. Its defects and mine too, increase as it ages.

I had never been taught to shoot, except by aiming at my own shadow, or diving in fear, or horse-riding except in dreams. I had no choice but to leap into the abyss, or become a traffic sign pointing to low places, suspicious areas, or an endless nebula.

In this nebula, and between the repression, my youth thrives. Girls from the wilderness occupy the imagination. The girls shimmering under the sun and scented with all the blossoms gathered by bees. Their occupation of the mind was not in vain. Each girl was created to smile from the moment of her birth cries until she is placed in her shroud. Like a dove that loves its dusty white feathers. She goes like sunlight from dawn, returning to her nest every evening, like other women. Their fortress has seven gates. How harsh it is for a lover to enter one of those gates that lead to a maze.

I wake up to the hum of my sewing machine, it is my beloved one made of iron. It leaves me every night, with my wounded worries, the pain of regret, absence, and loss.

Faces I no longer recognize appear, faces erased from my memory by harshness. My iron maiden only pays attention to its madness, recklessness, or indifference. My beloved from the tribe of iron, how many colorful threads have passed through her thread guides? How many coats more ragged than Gogol's have passed under its presser foot? These coats intersect with what has crossed its plate—fox fur with the howling of wolves in my head. How many times have those threads intertwined with ropes that drag me like a donkey through the streets of this era?

My beloved made of metal, entered that shrine as an angelic soul and emerged as scrap. It became like all the consumable things around us. Our tragedy lies in the beads of sweat that sometimes bloom far away from the field of spirit. That little iron instrument I once loved, taught it the games of war, chase and escape of money, men, and women. Yet, in all battles, I would always lose. No salvation came from a deceitful future or earthly paradise invaded by demons. Instead, hope intertwines between a present full of false promises and an empty future.

The lifetime decays behind this beloved machine that corrodes in a place that denies joy and repels literature and art—disciplines incapable of teaching moral values. Politics consistently fail to create beauty in our surroundings. The moment dissolves through time, desires fade into suppression, and hopes crumble with death. I am not hopeless; springs will cleave the rocks and burst forth.

CHAPTER NINETEEN

**The bird that falls into a trap is either
foolish or hungry.**

We were surprised by Grandpa Mustafa, who'd returned from Argentina and arrived at his son's house late at night without informing anyone.

My father asked him about his brother. Hamed had traveled with Mustafa from the beginning. During his previous visit, Mustafa told my father that Hamed was doing well and had no plans to return, so as not to experience a second sense of estrangement here. My father only knew his brother Hamed through a small faded photo in his wallet, which was worn by constant kisses and teardrops. My father was just one year old when his brother emigrated, never to return.

My mother also did not know her father Mustafa well because she was only two months old when he left. She'd only met him during his first visit back.

Grandpa Mustafa stared at my father a long time. Tears streamed down his cheeks. He wiped them with his fingers and let out a deep sigh that summarized his answer: "Your brother has passed away." With a choked voice, Grandpa simply added, "May you have a long life, and may God have mercy on him."

When Mustafa visited the next day to see my mother, no one had told him yet that she'd passed away as well. He was surprised by my father's new wife who introduced herself. He simply walked around our large house, the same place where he was born, raised, and married, turning his face away from us. He took a white cloth handkerchief from his pants pocket and wiped his tears. He was the only man in the village who wore pants and remained bareheaded.

Nothing is more burning than the tears of a regretful father who suppresses remorse, ignores guilt, or stifles the sobs caused by the loss of a loved one.

During Mustafa's first visit, my mother was the only one who made him feel the power of blood ties and kinship. He unleashed all his parental love upon her, the love she was initially deprived of. He also expressed his longing for the homeland he had left. But what would he do today?

He saw an empty home, devoid of both his only daughter and granddaughter, my younger sister, who carried our grandmother's name, Vida. She'd passed away just two months before this visit. Vida was the only female left with a trace of his departed daughter's scent. That alone was enough to change his answer to everyone's question: "Will you stay this time, or will you return to Argentina like your previous visit?"

Instead of saying, "Perhaps I'll stay" or "Maybe I'll stay," he remained silent.

As I was the sole confidant of his secrets, he would engage me in conversations about memories that had marked a sharp turning point in his life, shaking his soul and leaving him restless since. With tact and without hurting him, I'd encourage him to talk about his early youth in the village, his feelings toward women, and dormant memories that would reawaken within him. His confessions were like a spring, bursting forth after a rainy winter had soaked the earth following years of drought.

Upon his request, I accompanied him as we ventured into the countryside. We walked paths where his footsteps had not been recorded for a long time. His mind was present, and his memory never betrayed him. He named the places we visited, recognizing them regardless of changes that may have occurred since he'd last been there. It sometimes felt as if he had never left. At each location, he exclaimed: Oh, how many memories do I have here, with so-and-so at this place, or when I worked here or experienced this. His mind and memory were ablaze as we went on our daily journeys to places we did not often revisit.

One morning, while passing the village cemetery on our way to the countryside, we crossed a bridge above a water channel that divided the graveyard. The northern half held the remains of our family members and relatives. He suddenly stopped and pointed to one of the graves:

"Your grandmother was buried there. She died from the yellow wind, from the plague (cholera)."

Then, my grandfather stopped again. I noticed him staring at one of the graves. His eyes filled with tears, and he wiped them with the palm of his hand. I wanted to ask what made him so emotional, but he was faster to share his feelings.

"In that grave, my son, I buried a sweet rose that had once been an impossible dream..."

Sobs stole the rest of his words and choked them in his chest. He stopped talking. Tears flowed heavily down his cheeks and neck. He wiped them again.

We continued walking. Crossing another bridge, along a dusty path beside the canal on its southern side, we reached a point where the water flowed under a tunnel with a bridge above it. People crossed this bridge for work and other pursuits, and indeed village memories still linger there—a witness to an eternal story being told from times past.

I hesitated, then cautiously said: "No doubt the woman in that grave was significant to you. Perhaps the reason you couldn't marry her or her death prompted you to emigrate?"

He sighed.

"What saddens me my son is that she was killed because of a false accusation against her, passed on by someone to her older brother. At that time, the village had no more than 500 people, before I traveled to Argentina. Everyone in the village knew every little detail about each other, despite the presence of family rivalries that divided the village and tore its fabric apart during major and minor disputes. These disputes often occurred when appointing a village elder, a mayor, an official, a guard, or when someone violated one of the rare sanctities. Our small family was situated in the northern part of the village by virtue of residence and marriage alliances with the largest families on that side, who governed over the whole village.

"The girl who was killed—I had become attached to her before my mustache began to trace on my face. For two years, I couldn't get close to her and reveal my feelings for her. My attempts to meet her failed due to her living in another part of the village and her family's fierce protection of her reputation. Plus, she rarely went alone to the orchard or the water source by the canal. My heart ached in longing for her.

"One day, my father surprised me by saying, 'We will marry you off after harvest season!' I did indeed marry my cousin, who had been reserved for me since we were children. However, my mind still wandered to that girl."

As Grandfather paused in reminiscing, he struck his chest with his fist.

"Look at this old man before you. Look closely at me. Everything about me now speaks her name. Her image lodged in my head has never left me for a moment since those days up until now. She accompanied me through every step and everywhere I went—on ship journeys and during sleepless nights. She will remain with me until my last breath. I concealed this secret so as not to cloud the course of my life and the lives of those I live among.

"Your grandmother would always ask me, even in the early days of our marriage, 'Why are you always lost in thought?' I could tell her, 'I am in love!' But I stay silent. Even when I was in Argentina, I was like this. I married there three times, but remained loving the sweet rose like this; they wronged that innocent girl and killed her!"

Shyly, I tried to calm his agitation and console him.

"Many like her were unjustly killed," I said. "Hell will be filled with such criminals!"

He suddenly rose.

"Surely, I must precede them to hell because of my cowardice. Do you think a coward will enter paradise? No, a thousand times no. I should have done something and fought for her. Whoever cannot fight for what they love and who they love will not be qualified to enter paradise. Apart from their rightful losses on Earth.

God does not love cowards, nor does life; so, if there is hell and an afterlife, cowards in love will fuel its flames!"

He continued after a moment.

"There was one time when I wasn't a coward," he said.

His eyes drifted into the distance.

"When?" I asked.

"When I found myself empty-handed from every-thing and returned to the village after all these years!"

"But you returned, filled with what you saw in this world, experienced, witnessed, and suffered!"

"If I had known that I would be forced to travel to a country where I would live compelled to do ev-erything: understand a foreign language with others, communicate differently than the culture I was raised with, submit to norms that are not our nature—even though our nature and everything we are is mysterious to others—and lose family, neighbors, loved ones, and friends here, I would not have left for that country! Until now, immigrants, especially those in Argentina, cannot return to their homeland; all their life savings are not enough to cover the cost of travel. Thousands of migrants cannot return to their homes.

"There, they don't silence your mouth as they do in our country, nor do they treat you like slaves as they used to do in our land. There, you can say whatever you want in the face of all authorities. You can sleep with the woman you love. There, nothing stops you from doing anything!"

CHAPTER TWENTY

When you speak as a loving friend to the world,

you'll find that everything listens to you.

That day, I was not feeling well: anise season did not yield enough to cover the expenses; worst of all, the merchants played a game that affected all the farmers. A rumor circulated about the poor quality of the anise crop due to a disease, and the farmers believed it (it is generally known that anise has immunity against all plant diseases). As a result, the merchants acquired the season's produce at an extremely low price.

Many weddings and engagements were postponed until the following year. I went to the new workshop where I worked in Damascus. I saw the workers preparing to leave. When I entered the manager's office, he asked me to work evenings. Thus, I had to find a room to stay in since there would be no transportation to my village after midnight.

I went to an old man, in my profession, living in the western part of the Rose District. I asked about a room for rent. He assured me that my request would be granted. He invited me to sit opposite him while he worked away on a sewing machine. He stared at me as if we didn't know each other. He explained the conditions for renting the room, which I thought were a joke at first.

"The room is in the basement of a widow's house with three daughters; one of them is married but separated and lives with her mother. The other two are young and she is protective of them, even from a breath of air. The woman wants to rent a room in the basement apartment so that she and her daughters feel safe with a man protecting them.

"I trust you. Here are the conditions: When you come back from work, ring the outer bell twice and wait for at least two minutes, so they can get into their rooms; as there is only one kitchen in the apartment, which is shared between you and them. Also, in your room, there is a bell button that you must ring and wait for the same duration. The third condition: You're not allowed to have any visitors or let any relatives or friends know that you live here. As for the monthly rent, it's fifteen liras, given to me at the beginning of each month, and I will then hand it over to the woman. If you agree to this type of room and its conditions set by its owner, come now to meet her!"

I agreed before seeing the room for several reasons. First, its location near the Rose District. It was close to my work. Most importantly, it allowed me the opportunity to read and write without disturbance.

We headed to the place. The old man rang the bell. We waited the required time. The door opened, and the shadow of the person who opened it disappeared. We entered directly into the designated room. The room was well-lit and clean, with everything in it refreshing to the soul. It had a closed window, which seemed like it was never opened. It was covered with an airtight plastic cover, and a condition of staying there was not to open it. We entered and left without hearing any sound.

We returned to the old man's shop, and I paid him according to the terms, then left. I wasn't surprised by the situation because this city had been bearing darkness under various circumstances for centuries, with a history, unlike most cities in this world. The matter wasn't just about faith or what these women believed. It was about historical terror—referring here to Tamerlane's invasion of the Levant and the captive women there; this terror couldn't vanish at the same speed that fear fades from different stages: from Seljuk rule, Mamluk rule, Turks or French colonization.

Throughout the entire year, I did not violate any housing rules. I never saw a face or heard a voice. It was as if I were in a cell, without a guard. I left them without any regret. My consolation during that year in the house was learning everything about my mysterious girl in the Rose District neighborhood through an old painter who knew everyone. I kept a very small and blurry photo of her. I gave it to the painter with the pretext of him painting it in larger size for me. He raised a palm-sized magnifying lens and examined the picture. Slyly, he asked:

"Whose picture is this?"

"A girl I love."

"So, she's your girlfriend?"

He invited me to see his paintings while repeating phrases I believed he used often: "Some draw their lover with charcoal, oil, or on stained glass; and there are those who want to paint her on a flute, violin, or oud. I can embody other people's love. I'm a natural-born painter and like the picture, I am going to enlarge it in a painting, even if it's smaller than the head of a pin. All of that is easy for me."

Suddenly, he turned off the shop's lights. A sense of apprehension filled me. I feared this man who continued speaking.

"I can see other people's thoughts just as I see my own. You just need to look into my eyes as if you were looking at the person in the photo whom you want to enlarge."

Some of the paintings were covered. He unveiled a nearby canvas. "This woman thinks she is the Mona Lisa of her time," he said. "She's a pimp's companion. A man from outside the city requested that I paint the woman of his imagination, so this was the result. He was generous and paid the amount I asked for without hesitation or bargaining, hoping to return later and take the painting, but he left and never came back! I think he was afraid of something I don't understand."

I too began to feel fear creeping in deeper, but I composed myself and carried on. He headed toward the attic ladder and climbed up, commanding me in a tone of authority.

"Follow me to the tower. I call my attic, 'The tower.' Sometimes, I even convince myself that I'm really in a tower, but this illusion quickly fades, especially when distracted and my head hits one of the ceiling beams. The purpose of this beam is not to support the shop's roof but to wake me from my daydreams. I am constantly daydreaming, even as I walk through the market. Bumping into people all the time because of my absentmindedness, which results in numerous apologies: 'Excuse me, brother' or 'Excuse me, sir.' These two phrases are always on my tongue."

In the attic were abandoned drawings and colors. A stuffed hyena with truly frightening eyes was standing there. He joked and said: "Don't try to touch it; it might attack you!"

At that moment, my fear reached its peak, but I tried to be brave by not backing out from what I considered an adventure. There were also adorned paintings with various coverings, the material's value depending on their importance. Some were covered with silk; others with cotton fabric; some with perforated lace; and some with dirty burlap. He uncovered a painting with a silky cover and said, "Look closely. This is Carmen of this city."

He lifted the tattered burlap cover off another painting, "This is the fool of this city." And then a third painting, "I drew this one in secret lines that reveal themselves once it's touched. It's a picture of a foolish ruler who governed this city at some point."

Suddenly, there was a knock on the shop's front door.

"I'll show you more later after the customer who knocked on our door leaves," he said. "Follow me!"

We descended from the attic. The scarred young man at the door caught my eye with deep gashes on his face and neck, seemingly caused by a knife. Before the youth could ask for anything, the painter hurriedly handed him a remarkably colorful painting devoid of any scars. Seeing the painting, the young man furrowed his brow and angrily questioned the painter, "Is this me?!"

The painter looked at me hesitantly as if asking which was better: the portrait or the young man? I didn't know what to say or whom to side with.

The young man wanted his portrait with the scars, while the artist had removed those blemishes, thinking he'd done a good deed. The painter handed me the original black and white photo of the young man, no larger than an ID card. The young man looked like a criminal.

The youth refused to take the painting and slapped his hand on the table. Colored pencils fell from a glass cup that smashed to the floor. Panic struck the artist.

The young man said, "These scars are mine, and I'm not ashamed of them!"

"But I made it beautiful," said the painter.

"I came to you to enlarge my picture, not for plastic surgery!" Overwhelmed with his temper, he demanded another version.

"I want it ready by tomorrow!"

The painter nodded in compliance.

"I will try!"

"Don't say, 'I will try.' You said tomorrow, and tomorrow morning. I don't have time. Tomorrow I will leave for my distant town."

He left without looking back at us. I didn't reveal anything to the painter about my reactions, nor could I enter the world of that young man who aroused my curiosity. I wanted to know the source of his pride in the scars on his face and neck. They seemed repulsive to me.

The painter said, "What a strange world! And its wonders!"

It was as if the painter had realized something. He hurried after the young man and came back with a face still bearing signs of astonishment and bewilderment at the young man's attitude.

"He thinks that I can draw his deformities without touching them and looking closely at his scars.

Tomorrow his picture will be ready. I trust myself. When I stand behind the canvas, I feel like Picasso.

"We have thousands of events that are more important than the event that inspired his "Guernica" painting which immortalized it. I try, but there is no appreciation for art in this country; add to that our painters are lazy; but time knows how to put an end to the lazy person—it folds him without him realizing."

I checked my girl's picture. I made sure it was still in my pocket. She had once told me, "Two things will steal you: fear, and time!"

The painter said, "Come back tomorrow. I don't want to see your face around here!"

He said this with anger. I noticed it when he looked at the picture and returned it to me. I left the painter's studio with a cloud of sadness looming. I headed toward the entrance of the Rose District. I had to pass by the door of my mysterious girl's house. The door was closed. No face. No flower. No one. The world darkened in my eyes.

As soon as I laid my head on the pillow to sleep, the painter appeared in my dream like a sorcerer. I was terrified at first, but curiosity got the better of me, and I convinced myself to return the next day to witness his strange artistic magic. When I arrived, he smiled without responding to my greeting.

He said, "I'm amazed at how people treat time as if it were a handful of salty nuts to nibble or a loaf of bread to be divided."

He led me by the hand and climbed to the attic, where he stood before a white canvas and asked if I could see anything.

"I don't see anything," I said.

He laughed a long laugh while lines and colors formed within his laughter. Then he said, "You will see what you could never have expected."

In his hand was a brush resembling a thread of light, moving across the surface of the canvas. What was happening surpassed all astonishment; was I dreaming? Pinching my forehead with the palm of my hand—the painter appeared tense as he clutched the thread of light with his fingers. He looked at me and continued staring along with his finger movements while speaking words that were unimaginable:

"Time doesn't break down like a machine. There is no bad time, nor is there any other kind."

"There are people who left time to mock them!"

He asked me to look at the painting behind me. I turned around as he requested. I saw the picture of my Rose girl in her full height, turning her back to us.

"There is no hope from her!" he said.

In the painting, there was an awe that made me freeze from fear and anticipation.

"Stare into my eyes well," he said.

I was as if enchanted, looking at him. I felt a strange sensation taking over me. The arrival of the young man with scars, who promised to come that same day, saved me from this eerie and frightening situation. The young man climbed to the attic. He sat on a small wooden chair and leaned on a table nearby.

The painter said: "No picture for you before you tell us the story behind your scars."

Before starting to speak about himself, the young man wanted to know me, so I told him about the peripheral side of my life. The painter smiled and commented.

"There is no margin in a person's life! Today you will see what you consider unimportant and marginal; it was the driving force for your intellect, instincts, and emotions. Let's allow the young man to tell us his story about his scars. Pay attention to him well. He will be honest with every word he speaks."

The young man coughs, resting his cheek on the palm of his hand. He says, "I belong to a generation that jumped from its mother's womb into a bitter reality. Just like previous generations, we emerged from our mothers' wombs with clubs and axes in our hands to fight each other, even if we were brothers. Our town is far from civilization—as distant as Earth is from Mars—and far from the city. No one can hear needy cries coming from there. It sleeps with the sunset before the chickens do.

"The landlord allocates the plow to whomever he wants, whether it's a mule, a man, or a woman, simply to work. Everyone works for his benefit. One day, he put the plow on my father's back and told him he would cultivate the land like a donkey. I was just a child back then who hadn't experienced his childhood yet. Some days later, I gathered a group of children and we planned to wait for the landowner when he began punishing one of them. As soon as 'the punishment carnival' began and he placed the plow on the poor man's back, we attacked him and his assistants with stones. The landlord ordered our families to hand us over to him, and that's what happened.

"His deputy took me away, beating me until I fluttered like a sparrow between his hands. He pulled out and opened his folded knife and pressed the blade against my neck. The last sound I heard before losing consciousness was my mother's scream: 'My son!' From that moment on, her voice disappeared, along with her face, her tenderness, her warm hands, and her bread's taste—for she tried to save me from them but received her punishment in return! As the landlord said that dark day, immersed in destruction and torture, he banished our family from the town. Then we came to this city and lived here for years. I learned the mechanic profession and returned to the village to manage irrigation windmills after that landlord lost his authority over it."

The painter said to him: "That's enough for now."

The painter then turned to a framed canvas covered with a green silk scarf. He asked us not to approach it. He raised his hand above the canvas and removed the scarf with a trembling hand. The young man's wounds were reopened, gushing purple blood. The young man's face in the painting looked swollen, full of bruises. His eyes in the picture were burning with anger. The young man screamed with wonder of what he saw:

"That's me!"

He tried to approach the painting, but the painter stopped him.

"Stay back! Not until your wounds heal."

He turned to me, asking for the picture I wanted to enlarge in a painting. I slipped my hand into my jacket pocket. A shudder of fear took hold. I pulled out the trembling picture, and it stayed in my hand. The painter looked at me and studied my figure. Something shook me from within when he said: "You will not leave this place before you see the finished painting."

He went toward the opposite wall, lifted a black silk cover off a mounted canvas as tall as a person. The canvas was white. He asked us to close our eyes for a moment, as if we were small children, but we did not do that.

"No problem!" he said.

My eyes widened as I saw lines, colors, and expressions moving like light in the painting before settling down.

"It's her!" I said. "The girl from Rose District."

The girl squirmed within the frame of the painting.

She stared at me with sympathy and sorrow.

I lowered my head bashfully.

I saw her advance toward me.

I backed away until I hit the wall.

I wished I could vanish.

I was fragile compared to her vigor.

The girl noticed the flowing blood from the young man's wounds; she hurried toward his painting, tearing the cloth of her dress and wiping his wounds. Then she turned to us with her blood-stained hands. She passed me without looking back. She then stopped in front of the young man, while lowering her gaze modestly. She wiped the blood from her hands with her dress; then returned to check on the wounds. She removed the blood-soaked bandage and wiped it on her forehead, then gently touched the young man's wounds until they fully healed; later, she became engrossed in staring at his picture until she merged with its lines, colors, and eventually dissolved into it.

***

Glossary

Abu: Prefix commonly used meaning "father of".

Arak: A distilled alcoholic Middle Eastern drink made from grapes and aniseed, which gives it a licorice flavor.

Bey: Used as a courtesy title for a gentleman.

Bouhaird, Jamila: An Algerian heroine of the War of National Liberation from France, 1954–1962, known throughout the Middle East as "the Arab Joan of Arc.

Canopus: The brightest star in the southern constellation of Carina and the second-brightest star in the night sky.

Fez (hat): A felt headdress shaped like a short cylindrical, truncated hat, usually red, typically with a black tassel attached to the top.

Gendarmerie: A military force with law enforcement duties among the civilian population.

Ghajer: Our term for the nomadic Roma (gypsies). In Europe, Ghajer is a term the Roma use to refer to non-Roma.

Hejazi: A variety of Arabic spoken in the Hejaz region in Saudi Arabia.

Jalabiyas: A traditional, ankle-length loose-fitting, garment made of lightweight, flowing fabrics and worn in the Middle East by both men and women.

Jazira: The name Jazira is derived from the Arabic word for "island". Its meaning evolved to represent a geographic entity and a cultural and historical identity that transcends boundaries and spans different areas.

Jinn: Invisible creatures in early religion in pre-Islamic Arabia and have held space in Arab culture for almost as long as Arab culture.

Kohl-liner: Ancient eye cosmetic used around the eyes, primarily inside the row of eyelashes.

Maghrebi: Western Arabic; it includes the Moroccan, Algerian, Tunisian, Liyan, Hassaniya, and Saharan Arabic dialects.

Makdous: This ancient culinary delight stems from Syria. It consists of oil-cured baby eggplants and is stuffed with a mix of roasted red peppers, walnuts, garlic, salt, and olive oil.

Mehramah: Kerchief, a piece of fabric used to cover the head.

Sammaq Mountain: Also called Mount Summaq, It is located to the northwest of Idlib city in Syria.

Shaziliah: A traditional type of headscarf worn by local men in the countryside of Damascus.

Shemagh: A traditional type of headscarf worn by local men in Saudi Arabia and the Middle East.

Um: Prefix commonly used meaning "mother of".

Hsain Warour

Born on Dec 10th, 1941, also known as The Author Tailor, embarked on his multifaceted journey in the historic city of Damascus.

Coming from a humble peasant family in the suburbs, Hsain moved to Damascus at the young age of eleven to pursue his tailoring career. Learning from his skilled Armenian master, Vahram Shahbandarian, he honed his craft in Al-Khaja Souq of Damascus and went on to work in several clothing factories. Aside from his expertise in tailoring, Hsain had an unwavering passion for literature. Devoting much of his earnings to purchasing books, newspapers, and cultural magazines, Hsain cultivated a love for the written word that would soon blossom into his own creative pursuits. Remarkably, his first poetic experience was published in the Lebanese magazine Al-Maw'id when he was just fourteen years old.

We celebrate not only Hsain Warour's achievements as a tailor but also the depth and beauty of his literary contributions that remain an ongoing testament to his dedication, resilience, and passion for the arts.